Rebecca, Too

G. M. Lupo

Lupo Digital Services, LLC
Atlanta, GA

First edition (paperback).

ISBN: 978-0-9848913-8-2. Published by Lupo Digital Services, LLC, Atlanta, Georgia (www.lupo.net). Printed in the United States of America.

Acknowledgements

This novel began as an eighteen-page screenplay written at the request of Atlanta actor Michelle Kabashinski, who saw some pieces I had in a Sketchworks acting showcase around 2010. The script wasn't produced but the background I developed on the characters Alyssa and Rebecca formed the basis for the full-length play I wrote the following year.

The play was workshopped through Working Title Playwrights (WTP) in Atlanta and had a WTP On-Demand Reading (ODR) at Lionheart Theatre in Norcross, in May of 2013, directed by Tanya Caldwell with cast Erin Barr-Smith, Jessica McGuire, Abby Avery, Ryan McLaughlin, Jason Caldwell, Catherine Johns, Chuck Mason, Jamie Dion Hicks, Nancy Caldwell, Brooke Bishop, and Amy Syzmanski. Following this reading, the script took on much of the form it would be in when I began transforming it into a novel in 2017.

Daniel Carter Brown read and gave feedback on an early draft of the post-ODR version the play, and Hilary Rogers King read the before- and after-ODR versions and provided comments. Sigrid Economou, Carol Ippolito, Becky Hann Kraegel, and Leonard Pallats read an early draft of this novel in 2017, and offered feedback on it.

The play had a reading at Stage Door Players in Dunwoody (Artistic Director, Robert Egizio, Artistic Associate, Jacob York) in April 2018, directed by Julie Skrzypek with cast Maggie Birgel, Shannon McCarren, Cara Mantella, Trey York, Kerwin Thompson, Bryn Striepe, Bob Smith, Brittany Minnieweather, and Casey Gardner. Cast and audience feedback contributed to the development of the story portrayed here.

Jennifer Scott, Town Manager for Braselton, GA, and Cellar Door at Chateau Elan provided much helpful information.

Many thanks to Liz Dooley for editing and proofreading this novel, and to Melissa Mullaney for all your support.

Other Work by the Author

G. M. Lupo is the author of these works:

- Atlanta Stories: Fables of the New South
- Killing Babies: Collected Essays
- The Cheese Toast Project
- Freedom and Consequence
- The Long-Timer Chronicles

For new stories in development visit the author's blog Raised by Wolves at http://gmlupo.com.

G. M. Lupo can be found on the web at http://lupo.com.

To contact the author or to be added to the mailing list for future releases, send an email to author@gmlupo.com.

Once Upon a Time

Rebecca Asher leans her head back against the seat in the seafood restaurant where she's just finishing lunch, and rolls her eyes upward, as she listens to the inane conversation of the three girls seated behind her. She's in Fort Lauderdale for Spring Break 1999 and stopped in for a bite to eat. The trio behind her showed up just before her food arrived. For the past fifteen minutes, they've been discussing the relative "hotness" of *NSYNC versus Backstreet Boys and debating whether Joseph Gordon Levitt or James Van Der Beek would be the better prom date. As near as she's been able to deduce, they are Sandy, Mandy, and Andy, and given the proximity of their voices, it's Mandy and Andy seated just behind her with Sandy facing them. In addition to their ludicrous prattle, they frequently punctuate the conversation with loud gasps, giggles, and muted expletives, such as "oh my gosh" or "holy heck" prompting Rebecca to dub them "three little Christian girls running wild at Spring Break".

Of the three, it's the one they call Andy who annoys her the most. Her voice has a meandering and wavering quality to it, hardly modulating, with a hint of a Southern accent that suggests someone from the suburbs of a large city, rather than rural. Even when she's expressing a coherent thought, it sounds like she's rambling on about nothing. Rebecca is strongly tempted to step over to the table and lecture the three about Humphrey Bogart, Clark Gable, Robert Mitchum, and other "real men" from the Golden Age of Hollywood, who could more than obliterate the teeny-bopper idols they're fawning over — if she thought such a lesson would register with such obviously dim bulbs as these.

Rebecca has been in Fort Lauderdale for nearly twenty-four hours, arriving in the early afternoon the day before in the ancient, rust-bucket Toyota Corolla her mother purchased for her when she was learning to drive. Since it is Spring Break, all the hotels are booked, and even if they weren't, Rebecca could not afford the exorbitant prices quoted to her. She ended up in a "no-tell motel" a few miles from the strip, where she's the only patron booked for more than an hour at a time. She's certain that if it wasn't for the ratty condition of her car, she'd have already been robbed of the few possessions she brought with her, and, at the motel, as a precaution, she propped a chair under the door handle before she went to bed, having little confidence in the latch and deadbolt on the door, and remembered to take her bag with her when she left the room, though she's certain the cleaning staff is nonexistent.

The trip almost didn't happen; it wouldn't have if Rebecca had not totally defied her aunt, Rachel Lawson, who's been taking care of Rebecca and Steven since their mother, Sharon, died nearly two years before. Rachel is a nurse who specializes in the care of terminally ill patients, and, in the immediate aftermath of Sharon's death, Rebecca did find Rachel to be sympathetic and helpful in dealing with their shared grief. As she's learned to deal with the loss, however, she's come to view Rachel as over-protective and too cautious in not allowing Rebecca to explore her independence. When several friends proposed heading to Florida, Rachel expressed doubts that Rebecca was ready for such a trip without adult supervision and Rebecca's friends headed off without her. The following evening, Rebecca packed a bag, tossed it in the trunk of her car, and a few hours before sunrise, snuck out of the house and headed South. She has yet to hook up with her friends in Fort Lauderdale and has started to suspect they went to Orlando instead.

Her thoughts are interrupted by the sound of something dropping to her right. Investigating, she discovers that the purse of one of the chatty girls behind her has slipped down beside the seat. She listens for any indication that the girl — Rebecca is certain it's the one called Andy — has noticed it missing, but she's currently rattling on about something to do with Dawson's Creek, and sounds as though she's leaning away from Rebecca, who slides over and slips her hand beside the seat, just able to get her fingers onto the purse. Slowly, she draws it to her, then sets it discreetly on her lap and peers inside, finding it full of makeup, pens, a checkbook, and a wallet that seems crammed with cash or credit cards.

Just then, in the middle of a discussion of all the "awesome" things they'll be doing today, she hears Andy say, "Where's my purse?" The question is ignored by the girl who seems furthest from Rebecca, so Rebecca stuffs the purse into her bag, slides her bag over her shoulder, tosses some cash onto the table to cover her meal, then slides out of her seat, and heads toward the door. The Braves jersey she has on, with the number ten — Chipper Jones's number — catches the attention of the girl facing her, who calls after Rebecca, "Chipper!" Rebecca ignores her and walks out and around the side of the restaurant. She makes sure she's not visible from the door, then takes her time in rifling through the purse.

At last, she finds a driver's license, with the name "Alyssa

Ruth Walker" and, for a moment, Rebecca can't figure out how they derived "Andy" from that. She finally decides it must be so her name will match those of her friends, which further lowers Rebecca's opinion of the trio. Alyssa's photo shows a blonde girl with a pleasant smile — Rebecca definitely finds her attractive — and an address in Lawrenceville, not far from where Rebecca lives in Decatur, which explains Alyssa's accent. The next thing to catch Rebecca's eye is Alyssa's birthdate, April 20th, 1981. The same as hers. As she suspects, the wallet is full of money, and an American Express card issued to Paxton Walker, who Rebecca surmises is Alyssa's father. She wonders if Alyssa is responsible enough to report the card lost once she returns to her hotel, or if she'll spend an extended time trying to find it, which would give Rebecca the opportunity to purchase quite a bit. Looking back to the photo, then the birthdate, however, another thought crosses her mind. She puts the license into her pocket, replaces the wallet in the purse, and stuffs it into her bag.

Rebecca moves back toward the front of the restaurant and peers through the window at the table where she was sitting. A black girl and an Asian girl are standing at the booth near hers, while a blonde girl Rebecca now recognizes as Alyssa frantically searches around the booth. After several minutes, the other girls convince her to leave and they head out to the street, Alyssa still upset. Rebecca follows them at a discrete distance, formulating in her head how she can use the missing purse to work her way into whatever plans the three girls have.

Tim Caine is seated at the bedside of his wife, Alyssa, staring intently at her. It's evening, 22 August 2010, and he's dressed in shorts, a polo shirt and sneakers, and is wearing a Seattle Mariners baseball cap turned backwards. He's been a steady presence at Alyssa's bedside at Grady Hospital in downtown Atlanta ever since she was moved to a private room upstairs, from the emergency ward, following the intervention of her sister, Leah. Alyssa has been at Grady for less than a week following a car accident near where they live in John's Creek, while she was headed home from the school where she teaches. The accident occurred on their first wedding anniversary and Tim had been on the phone with her a few minutes before she crashed, which, the police said happened as she was trying to avoid another accident. Since she's been moved, Tim has split the duty of staying with Alyssa with Leah, who typically takes the night shift, while Tim stays during the day. He's taken vacation time from his work as a loan officer for a credit union to be here, and hopes she comes out of her coma soon, as he's almost exhausted all his time off for the year.

It has been a particularly rough month for the family, starting with the death of Alyssa's father, Paxton Walker, in early August, of a heart attack while he was golfing. Alyssa was devastated by her father's death, which meant that making the arrangements for his funeral fell to Leah, who had a seriously strained relationship with their father. While this had been a source of tension for the sisters, everyone agreed that Leah handled her responsibility admirably, and gave their father a fitting send off. Alyssa had been particularly grateful, so much so that Tim sensed the sisters would successfully get past whatever difficulties they had endured. He hopes to have Leah over once Alyssa's back on her feet to suitably thank her for all she's done.

The door opens, and Leah enters with a book under her arm. Tim looks in her direction, then rises to greet her. Leah is average height, with dark auburn hair and intense blue eyes. Tonight, she's dressed in shorts and an old MIT sweatshirt, eschewing her usual business attire.

"How's she doing?" Leah asks.

"About the same," Tim says. "Thank you, once again, for getting her into this room. Way less chaotic than where they had her downstairs."

Leah holds up her hand. "It's the least I could do. The Walker Foundation has given Grady a lot of funding since the early-nineties. If that's not worth special consideration once in a while, I don't know what is."

"Well, I really appreciate it," Tim says. "There's no way our insurance would have covered a private room." He eyes the book Leah has. "What did you bring?"

"Grimm's Fairy Tales," Leah says, displaying the book. "It was one of Alyssa's favorites as a child."

"Sounds great," he says. He gives Leah a quick hug. "See you in the morning." He heads out.

Leah goes to the bed and kisses Alyssa on the forehead. "It's just you and me, Princess." She holds up the book. "Brought one of your favorites, tonight." She sits and begins reading. Fifteen or twenty minutes after Tim leaves, Nurse Angelique steps into the room. Speaking to her at the nurses' station outside, Leah learned Angelique is originally from the Ivory Coast and studied in Haiti, and this gave Leah the opportunity to say some words in French before she went in to visit Alyssa.

"It is kind of you to read to your sister all night," Angelique says in French.

"I am fortunate that my business can sometimes function without me," Leah replies. She watches as Angelique performs her examination. "Have the doctors given any indication when she might awaken?"

"They have not discussed her condition with me," Angelique says. "I can only see what they write in the system." She takes a long look at Alyssa. "But I feel she will awaken soon. All her test results are positive. She is lucky to be in good condition."

"My sister is in very good shape," Leah says. "She is a distance runner."

Angelique nods. "Yes. I can see she is well-conditioned. That will work in her favor."

Angelique concludes her examination and makes small talk with Leah for a moment longer before excusing herself to visit another patient.

"Come on, Princess, we need you back," Leah says. "Your sister misses you." She stares at Alyssa a long moment before opening the book and proceeding to read aloud. Concentrating on her reading, Leah does not notice when Alyssa's breathing increases, and her eyes suddenly begin rapidly darting from side to side under her eyelids.

Rebecca crosses the border from South Carolina to Georgia on Interstate 85 in her copper-colored Mini Cooper, the morning of 29 November 2005, headed toward her hometown of Atlanta. She's returning from a film festival she was covering in Greenville, anxious to get back home, unaware she has less than an hour left to live. The festival was not a pleasant experience for her and her harsh appraisal of it on her blog is only just now starting to register with organizers there, who are very upset with her criticism. She spent the whole trip under a cloud, in fact, having had a major falling out with someone for whom she cares deeply a few days before she left.

The past few years have been challenging for Rebecca, since leaving school in New York and trying to regroup back in her hometown. She had been in her junior year at Columbia University, and doing well, when her estranged father decided to insert himself back into her life, for which she was unprepared and handled badly, relying on booze and marijuana to deal with the negative emotions brought on by the encounter. This led to her failing all her classes and being placed on academic probation. When she arrived back in Atlanta, her problems were exacerbated by a feud she initiated with her aunt. Recently, Rebecca replaced Rachel as Steven's guardian, and that has given Rebecca a renewed sense of stability. She has recently been looking into resuming her studies at Georgia State University. Now, she only needs to repair the damage with Claire — the friend with whom she had her falling out — to get everything back on track.

Seeing a sign announcing the exit for the town of Braselton, an amusing thought crosses Rebecca's mind. Many years before, the Georgia actor, Kim Basinger reportedly bought the entire town and Rebecca has an idea to stop in for a look around, then maybe head to Chateau Elan for lunch and a tour of the winery.

She takes out her phone and dials Steven to give him a first-hand assessment of the festival. In a voice emulating the cadence of actress Bette Davis from *All About Eve*, Rebecca says, "Oh — my — god, Stevie, it was horrible!"

"That bad, eh?" Steven says.

"Whoever told Greenville to sponsor a film festival should be tied to the whippin' post."

"Why don't you tell me how you really feel, Becky?"

"Seriously, who has their closing ceremonies on Monday?"

"I was wondering why you stayed the extra day," he says. "Think you'll be back by lunch?"

"No. I'm taking a detour into Braselton," she replies.

"Braselton?" Steven says, amused.

"Thought I'd look around and try to figure out what Kim Basinger saw in it all those years ago," she says.

"Sounds like an adventure."

"Hey, dinner tonight, okay? I'll give you all the gory details — heavy emphasis on gory."

"I can't wait," Steven replies.

"Later Goonie."

Rebecca gets off the Interstate and takes Highway 53 into Braselton. The main attractions are some antebellum homes, one of which appears to be an event space. She pulls in at a merchandise mart near the intersection of Highway 124, which leads toward the winery, and takes a smoke break as she window-shops outside the antiques mall. She notes that Mayfield Dairy offers tours as well as an ice cream shop but decides against stopping there.

Finished with her tour, she hops onto Highway 124 for the trip to Chateau Elan. Once she's on her way, she dials Claire, and gets a recording. "Hey babe. Listen, I know I sound like a broken record, but we really need to talk. I sent you a video, explaining myself, and I hope you didn't just delete it. I'll be home this evening if you want to come over. Stevie's there, so we won't be alone. You know I love you — my Clarabella. I mean it! I was an idiot, okay. Could we start again, please?"

Rebecca finishes the call and drops her phone into the cup holder. Her attention is drawn by a semi-trailer weaving in its lane as it speeds toward her. "What the hell are you doing truck driver?" The truck suddenly crosses into her lane. She barely has time to shriek "Oh my god!" before being slammed toward the steering wheel, as the airbag deploys. She's stopped by the seat belt, then thrust violently backward as the front of her vehicle crumples, and the cab of the truck rips through her car, crushing every bone in her body and throwing her into darkness, before she can even feel any pain. Her last thought is a vision of her brother, that flashes, before all perception ceases.

Alyssa trudges through a dense forest, wearing a long, flowing, satin gown with puffy sleeves, that's tattered, worn, and dirty. On her feet are battered slippers, totally inappropriate for the rocks and dirt and crushed leaves and sticks she's walking on. She sees no sign of civilization, but in the distance can hear what sounds like drumming or pounding and detects in the air the faint smell of smoke. Something about the location feels familiar to her, but she doesn't recognize where she is. She has no idea how long she's been here or how she got here. All she remembers is walking and walking. She's thankful she's a runner, and trains a lot, otherwise she's not sure how much she could handle of this.

She searches her memory for what she'd been doing prior to finding herself in the woods, but no images, sounds, smells, or other indications come to her, which she finds unusual, since she has a photographic memory. All she can recall are miles and miles of wooded area. At last, she rounds a bend and comes into a small clearing that's dotted with granite boulders. Sitting on one of the rocks is a man of average height, a little on the heavy side, with long, brown hair, and a dark beard with silver slivers throughout that's neatly trimmed. He's wearing black cargo shorts with hiking boots, and a faded blue hoodie over top of a red T-shirt. He tracks Alyssa with his eyes as she moves into the clearing. She stops, and they face off in silence for several moments.

"Welcome, Princess," he finally says. "I've been waiting for you." Questions flood into Alyssa's head at once. The man smiles. "So many questions. Which to ask first? Let me help you."

Alyssa's head clears, and a question comes to her. "What is this place? Where am I?"

"You don't recognize it?" he says. "We're near the largest exposed outcrop of granite in the world. You and your track team sometimes ran here on weekends in high school."

"Stone Mountain?" Alyssa says. "We usually ran around the lake."

"Lake's not here, yet," he says. "No Army Corps of Engineers to build it. We'd actually be in the middle of it now if it was here." He points to a moderate sized creek. "There's one of the waterways they're going to dam up to create it."

"What do you mean by that?" she says. "How can we be here before the lake gets created?"

"We aren't in the current day," he replies. "This is about three hundred years before the Creek Secession. You read about that in your Georgia history class, remember?" He chuckles. "Use that wonderful photographic memory I gave you to access the details." He points behind her. "There's a tribal settlement about a mile in that direction, but we won't be going there. They're going to have enough problems with white settlers in the future, including our ancestors unfortunately." He looks around. "When I think of all the species that have been driven to extinction from this time to ours. Wish I could conger up some Passenger Pigeons, but I don't really know what they looked like or how they behaved. Oh well."

"How is this possible?" Alyssa asks.

"Anything's possible in this universe, Princess," he says. "I had to bring you here because we need to talk and, other than a few scattered allusions to taunt the readers, I don't exist in your world."

"Look, do me a favor. If we're going to talk, call me by my name," she says. "No one calls me Princess anymore."

"Someone still does," he says.

"Yeah, my sister, Leah," Alyssa says. "It drives me up the wall when she calls me that."

"Not always," he says.

"How do you even know that?" Alyssa asks.

"I know everything there is to know about you, Princess," he says. "You have lived inside my head for many years."

"That's more than a little creepy," she says. "How do I know you're not some looney serial killer out here toying with me?"

He reacts with frustration. "If I was going for sinister, I'd have put the hoodie up, okay? It's not easy playing god. I'm trying to be a little mysterious. Work with me here."

"Okay. Who are you?" Alyssa says. "Let's start there."

"I am the hand of fate, Princess," he says, "the all-seeing eye in the sky; myth maker, spinner of yarns, that man behind the curtain, twister of truth." He rises and bows to her, "The story-teller — at your service."

"That makes things as clear as mud," Alyssa says.

"If you need a name, call me Benjamin," he says.

"That's my grandfather's name," Alyssa says. "Benjamin who?"

"You know this one, Princess," he says. "Benjamin is a ravenous wolf. By day he devours the prey; by night he divides the spoils."

"That's from Genesis," Alyssa recalls. "The sons of Israel. So, your name's not really Benjamin, is it?"

"Stop worrying about my name. It'll be on the cover," he says. "That's not why you're here."

"Hold on," she says. "I think I get this. You brought me here. You gave me my photographic memory. How can you even be here? Doesn't that make you—"

"It's a perfectly valid literary convention," he says.

"I guess. You say you brought me here? How? Why?" Alyssa says. "Why am I dressed like this?"

He shakes his head with a sigh. "You should have already figured out the significance of the dress. You're a teacher, for crying out loud. As for how you got here, perhaps a little context is in order. Fasten your seatbelt, Princess. Things are about to get very bumpy."

Alyssa, twenty-nine, drives her red Honda Odyssey along Peachtree Parkway headed toward her home in John's Creek, Georgia. It's late afternoon, 18 August 2010, and Alyssa has been at school all day. She's just getting back to class, late, due to her time off following the death of her father, Paxton, earlier in the month. Her husband, Tim, has promised her a night out to celebrate their first wedding anniversary. She takes out her phone and speed dials her husband, placing the phone on speaker.

"Aly are you headed toward home?" Tim says.

"Yeah, Tim — running late as usual," she says. "Don't worry. I'll be back in plenty of time for whatever anniversary surprise you've cooked up for us tonight."

"Not a problem," he says. "I made the reservations for midnight."

"Ha. Ha. Very funny."

"How was class?" Tim asks.

"School was okay," she says. "I've missed being around the kids, so now that I'm back in my routine, things are finally starting to feel more normal."

"That's good. Just remember, I'm here for you. Love you."

"I love you too, honey. See you soon."

Alyssa disconnects and stares at her phone a moment, recalling there's someone she's been meaning to contact, Steven Asher, the brother of someone she once knew. She speed-dials the number she found on the Internet for him but gets a recording. "Hi, ah, Steven. This is Alyssa Caine. You don't know me but — Gosh, I was hoping I'd be able to actually talk to you. I'll give you a call back a little later, okay? It's about — it's about Rebecca. Talk to you then."

Alyssa finishes the call. She's startled as, ahead, two cars collide, and one skids into her lane. She screams, "No!" and jerks the wheel to the side, losing control of the vehicle. She senses as it leaves the road then feels a terrible jolt, and all goes dark.

Alyssa snaps back into the clearing, terribly shaken. "What's going on here? Am I dead? Is this heaven — or the other place?"

"You're not dead," the man says. "With any luck, you'll outlive me by a very long time."

"Let's cut to the chase," she says, borrowing one of her sister's favorite phrases. "Why did you bring me here? What was that accident all about? Was it real?"

"It was as real as things get in your world, Princess," he says.

"Then I must assume I survived," she says. "If I'm not dead."

"You're not dead, but you're pretty banged up," he says. "This, too, shall pass."

"So, why am I here with you?" Alyssa says. "Why have you chosen to insert yourself into the story?"

"Some connections need to be made," he says. "People need to come together; fates need to intertwine. You know, all that literary crap."

"How am I a part of that?" Alyssa says.

"You're the catalyst," he says.

"Why me?" she says.

"You just are, okay?" he says. "The whole Expanded Universe is in flux. Every time some new element gets introduced, the story gets more complicated. In retrospect, maybe I should have figured out the basic story first, instead of adding in all the fairy tale crap, but we have to work with what we have at this point."

"Okay, I'm not even going to try to follow all that," Alyssa says. "What do you need from me?"

"You're going to need to go a little crazy for a few days," he says. "Freak out your family, that kind of stuff."

"Why?"

"Because time is short, and we need to expedite things," he says. "That's why you're here now. The narrative is going to become very complex and I need to be sure it's clear in your head, even though things will seem a little nutty from your perspective."

She takes a seat on a boulder and speaks in a resigned voice. "I guess there's no way around this. Go ahead."

"Oh, good," he says. "Try to follow along as best you can. It doesn't always make sense to me either. It's a basic fairy tale motif. Two sisters have lost one another and must reunite."

"That seems easy enough," she says.

"Nothing's ever easy in fairy tales, and you know that," he says, "or fiction for that matter."

"Get on with it," she says waving her hand.

"Okay, so the sisters are lost and need to find one another," he says. "But one has also become enchanted."

"Oh, of course," she says. "Can't imagine who."

"To break the spell, she must complete three tasks," he says. "In no particular order, protect the boy, reconcile with the fair maiden."

"And confront the dragon, am I right?" Alyssa says.

"How'd you figure that out?" he says.

"There's always a dragon," she says. "I've studied Bettelheim."

"Ah, right," he says. "I should have remembered that. Too many revisions."

"Do I have to do all this on my own?" Alyssa says.

"No. You should seek to reconnect with the Divine Feminine for assistance," he says.

"I don't even know who or what that is," Alyssa says.

"Sure, you do," he replies. "Behind her back, you call her the Sorceress."

"Leah," she murmurs. "But, if I reconnect with my sister, doesn't that complete the tale?"

"You'll be enchanted, remember?" he says. "You have to break the spell first."

"Oh, right," she says. "Who is this boy I'm supposed to protect? How do I find him?"

"This one I'll give you, mainly because you've already found him," the man says. He mimics Alyssa on the phone, "Hi, ah, Steven. This is Alyssa Caine. You don't know me, but—"

"Steven Asher," Alyssa says. "He's in his twenties. He's hardly a boy."

"You'll catch on," the man says. "As for the others, you'll figure those out as you go along. We've reached a critical juncture. So many lives are about to change. So many destinies are about to be altered. You have to be the agent of that."

"Again, why me?" she says.

"You were the first," he tells her. "Before Leah; before even Rebecca." He turns and spreads out his arms. "In trying to tell your story, I crafted an entire universe and populated it with all manner of fascinating characters. Without you, none of it would have existed."

"No pressure, eh?"

"Your name wasn't always what it is now, but you have always been blonde; you have always been taller than average; you have always been athletic," he says. "You've always been married to Tim, though he's undergone a lot of changes as well — and your story always starts with a crash."

"I've lived inside your head for many years," she says aloud but to herself.

"I can't explain it any more succinctly than that, Princess," he says. "I can, however, give you a gift to help you along."

From all around her, Alyssa hears a voice. "Hello, Princess."

Alyssa looks around. "Mama?"

"No," the man says. "That's you; voice of your subconscious, if you will. It's an honest mistake. I don't think you realize how much you sound like your mom. You'll also be accompanied by a friend."

Rebecca Asher, as she looked when Alyssa met her in Florida, appears from out of the woods and joins them. Alyssa covers her mouth with her hands. "Becky? You're alive."

"Only in your memory, Aly," Rebecca says then vanishes.

"I think that just about covers it," the man says.

"Wait. If I ask you an unrelated question, will you answer me honestly?" Alyssa says.

"As honestly as I can, Princess," he says.

"Will Tim and I have children?" Alyssa says. "We're putting it off, but we worry sometimes if we'll ever be ready."

"You certainly will." He seems to debate something with himself. "Oh, I don't see any harm in it. You'll only remember this as a dream." He points to another part of the clearing, where a young teenage girl and a pre-teen boy step out through the trees.

Both are mixed race and bear similar features to others in Alyssa or Tim's families. The man presents them. "Meet Sarah Naomi and Gerald Paxton Caine."

"They're beautiful," Alyssa says, her eyes brimming with tears.

She tries to approach them, but the man stops her. "No, no. You can't interact with them. Not yet."

"Why not?" Alyssa says, disappointed.

"Their existence is a fact, but their stories have yet to be written," he says. "Do you understand?"

Alyssa nods. "I think so. Yes."

"Let me assure you — nothing that happens in the next few days will prevent them from being here when their times come," he says. The young people vanish.

"Thank you," Alyssa says.

The man says, "Is there anything else?"

"Will I see you again?" Alyssa asks.

"I'll be around in some small form or another," he says. "But as I said, for the most part, I don't physically exist in your world. I sort of take care of things behind the scenes."

"I understand," she says.

"Okay, then." He steps in front of her and places his hands on her shoulders, kisses her on the forehead, and stares into her eyes. "Time to wake up, Princess."

Snapshot McCall

Nurse Lana Turner moves down the hall of the private ward at Grady Hospital in Atlanta her workplace of nearly-twenty years. In that time, she's seen the job move from patient charts on clipboards hung on the foots of beds to sophisticated, hand-held devices that automatically update the central database, showing up in the patient care system where doctors can chart the course of treatment on a given patient and make recommen-dations on restorative procedures. Despite the technological advances, the one aspect that remains the same is the human element. Patients and their loved ones want a friendly face and a reassuring voice to help them through a medical emergency, and Lana always strives to be just that.

She pauses outside the room of Alyssa Ruth Caine, a young woman in her twenties, brought in the previous Wednesday with head trauma following a car accident in Peachtree Cor-ners. According to her husband, Tim, she lost control of her car trying to avoid another accident and crashed into a wall. Her seat belt and airbag saved her life, but the impact shook up her brain, causing swelling. Tim also said Alyssa recently lost her fa-ther and is a schoolteacher with a sweet and loving disposition. Whenever she's there alone with Alyssa, Lana always gives her words of support and encouragement.

On several occasions, Lana's had to deal with Alyssa's older sister, Leah, a difficult woman, who strikes Lana as the typical, pushy, well-to-do white woman, who thinks everyone's sup-posed to drop everything and pay attention when she speaks. Average in height, with a medium build, and reddish-brown hair, she has piercing, steel-blue eyes which she often focuses on someone for a long moment before uttering, "Perfect!" — her favorite phrase, Lana has concluded — often with more than a hint of sarcasm, and insists everyone on staff call her Doctor Walker, even though she's not a medical doctor. Lana is certain that causes confusion in the hospital but honors the request. Doctor Walker asks a lot of detailed questions and is very quick to escalate issues if she feels she's not getting an appropriate level of attention. Most of the people on staff prefer dealing with Tim, who's been a sweetheart the entire time.

Lana makes a quick notation on her pad to close out the pre-vious patient, switches to Alyssa's record, then enters the room. Tim is seated, asleep, at Alyssa's side, holding her hand. His skin is medium-toned, and he has a trim, athletic build, and a few days' growth of beard. His facial features put Lana in mind of Nigerians she met on her trip to Africa a few years ago, particularly those of the Yoruba tribe. In talking to him, Lana has learned he's originally from the West Coast and decided to stay in Atlanta after finishing school at Mercer, and that he and Alyssa met through an outdoors group that sponsors hiking and camping trips for busy singles with a love of nature. Lana spoke to him about Leah, but he assured her, "Don't read too much into her act. She's like that with everyone."

While she's never seen Alyssa on her feet, Lana can see she's well above average in height and slender in build. Tim has mentioned she's a distance runner, who also enjoys cycling, and swimming. Fortunately, the accident did not necessitate cutting her hair, which is long and very blonde.

Tim stirs. "Morning, Lana. How's she looking?"

"Morning, Tim," she replies. "Not much has changed. The doctors say she could come out of it any time. I take it Alyssa's sister left."

"Yeah, Leah headed home to get some rest," he says. Tim rises and stretches. "I'm going to get some coffee. Maybe a bite to eat." He exits.

Nurse Turner concludes her examination, and steps away from the bed to make notations on her electronic device. Suddenly, Alyssa groans. Lana turns to see Alyssa's eyelids fluttering, and her head moves back and forth on the pillow. She groans again, then raises her right hand to her head. She opens her eyes. Slowly, and in a breathy voice that puts Lana in mind of an old movie star, Alyssa says, "Oh — my — god. What happened? Where am I?"

Lana puts away the electronic device and moves to the bedside. "Ms. Caine? Can you hear me? Alyssa?"

"Of course, I can hear you," Alyssa says in a very agitated voice. She puts her hands up to shoo Lana away. "I'm right here. Who's Alyssa?"

"You are," Lana says. "How are you feeling?"

"Like JFK in the Zapruder film," Alyssa says.

"That's to be expected — I suppose — after what you've been through." The first notion to come to Lana is that this does not sound like the Alyssa Tim has described. She almost sounds like her sister who Tim says she's nothing like.

Nurse Turner raises the bed and as she does, Alyssa glances at Lana's name badge. She chuckles. "Lana Turner? Is that the name you were born with?"

"It sure is," Lana says.

"Your parents had a sense of humor," Alyssa says.

Lana finds this amusing. "Actually, I was named after my aunt. Her parents had the sense of humor."

Alyssa looks again at the name tag and seems confused. "Wait, does that say Grady? Why'd they bring me back to Atlanta?"

"It was the closest available trauma center to where the accident occurred," Lana says. "You were just a few miles away and in pretty bad shape."

"I'd hardly call Braselton a few miles away." Alyssa places her hand to her head again. "Oh, my head! Listen, is my brother Steven here?"

Lana gives Alyssa a curious look. "I don't know your brother. Your husband Tim is here. He just went to the cafeteria."

"Husband?" Alyssa says. "Hello! Not married, Lana."

Nurse Turner steps away from the bed. "I'm going to get the doctor."

"Oh yeah? Who's he? Clark Gable?" Alyssa says.

Nurse Turner shakes her head, then exits.

Once in the hallway, she sees Tim exit the men's room and head for the elevator. She hurries toward him and calls out, "Tim? Tim!"

He turns.

"Alyssa's awake," she says. "I'm going to get the doctor."

"Thank god," Tim says as he jogs toward the room.

Alyssa, in a panicked state, walks with her friends Sandy and Mandy back to their hotel. They just had lunch at a seafood restaurant nearby and Alyssa's purse went missing. They'd been in the middle of a very animated conversation when she looked beside her, and realized it was gone. Neither Sandy nor Mandy could remember her having it, but Alyssa knows she brought it. She can remember every detail of her preparations to go to the restaurant, taking a shower, careful not to get her hair wet, picking out her pink top, white shorts and suede loafers, staring at the phone and wondering if she should call her father to check in and deciding against it, and finally putting her purse over her right shoulder. She clearly remembers having it there as she sat in the booth and moving it from between her and Mandy once they were seated, leaning it against the wall by her left hip. Then, it was gone. She searched around, beside and under the bench she was on, but it was nowhere.

"Purses don't just disappear," Sandy told her as she searched. "Come on, Miss Memory, you must have left it in the hotel room."

"I know that I didn't," Alyssa replies. "I'm supposed to pay for lunch. That has all my cash in it."

"You just want to get out of paying the tab, that's all," Mandy said. She and Sandy laughed.

"Look, we're going to go back to the hotel and it will be there, and you're going to feel really silly," Sandy assured her.

Prior to leaving the restaurant, Alyssa checked with their server, and at the register, and asked to speak to the manager, who said no one had turned in a purse, but that he'd keep an eye out for it. The whole way back, Alyssa is preoccupied with it and once they arrive back at the hotel, as she predicted, it isn't in their room. They have plans to hit the strip and check out whatever events are being sponsored that afternoon. Alyssa tells Mandy and Sandy to go ahead without her, while she retraces her steps.

"We should help you look," Mandy says.

"No. Seriously. I don't want you to miss out on any fun while I try to figure this out," Alyssa says. "If I find it, I'll meet you at the beach, otherwise, I'll contact the police and report it lost, then arrange to have Daddy wire me more money and cancel the card. We can hook up later."

Reluctantly, Mandy and Sandy agree, and, following a group hug, they head off to the beach. Alone in the room, Alyssa closes her eyes and tries to recreate her steps. She walks through everything she remembers from earlier. Assured she walked out of the room with her purse, she exits and heads down to the lobby, where she checks in at the front desk. No one has turned in a purse. She steps away from the desk and pounds her head with her fist. "Stupid, stupid."

From nearby comes a woman's voice with an indistinct accent that puts Alyssa in mind of how people speak around Atlanta, "Alyssa Ruth Walker?"

Alyssa looks to see a short, dark-haired girl, about her age, wearing shorts and a Braves jersey, approaching, holding what looks like a driver's license. Over one shoulder, she has a carry-all bag. Alyssa raises her hand. "That's me."

The girl stops and retrieves Alyssa's purse from her carryall and holds it up. "Lose something?"

A strong sense of relief washes over Alyssa. She hurries to the girl, takes the license and purse, and gives her an exaggerated hug. "Yes! Oh my gosh. Where did you find it?"

"I was having lunch at Barnacle Bill's and it was wedged beside my seat," the woman says.

"I knew I took it to the restaurant," Alyssa says. "That's so weird. I searched all around my seat."

The woman looks away from her. "Well, I guess you must have missed a spot." A thought seems to come to her. "Oh. You better check and make sure everything's there. Just in case somebody grabbed it."

Alyssa rummages through the purse. "Yep. Everything seems to be here." She positions the purse over her neck so that it hangs under her left arm and extends her hand. "I'm Alyssa, but I guess you already know that. My friends call me Aly."

"Aly?" the woman says in a tone that sounds slightly surprised. "Aly. Of course." She takes Alyssa's hand. "I'm Rebecca. Becky."

"Nice to meet you, Becky," Alyssa says. "You just saved me from an enormous amount of hassle."

"It's funny," Rebecca says. "I was just going to turn it in at the register, but decided to check for a license, in case you were still in the restaurant. I noticed you live near Atlanta and were born April 20, in '81. That's when I was born."

"So, you are from Atlanta," Alyssa says, to which Rebecca nods. "I thought I recognized the accent. Any idea which hospital?"

"My mother said Northside," Rebecca says.

"That's where I was born," Alyssa says. "We were there together and had to come all the way to Florida to meet."

They laugh. Rebecca says, "Listen, do you have any plans? There's a coffee shop nearby that has acoustic shows in the afternoon. I was thinking of checking it out."

"I'm planning on meeting up with my friends, but I have some time." Alyssa links her arm into Rebecca's. "The coffee shop sounds wonderful."

They head toward the door.

"Oh," Rebecca says. "I'm a little short on cash. I'll need to hit an ATM along the way."

"Don't worry about it," Alyssa says. "My treat. For finding my purse."

"I won't argue with that," Rebecca says.

Rebecca sits up in the hospital bed, watching as the nurse exits. *What the hell is going on here?* A blonde girl, who appears to be around ten, sits cross-legged at the end of the bed. She's been there throughout the exchange with the nurse, watching everything with fascination. Rebecca wonders why the nurse didn't mention her. Once the nurse goes, Rebecca focuses all her attention on the girl. Something about her seems familiar, but the woman she resembles is Rebecca's age, not a young girl.

"Who are you?" Rebecca says.

"I am you as you are me," the blonde girl says, then giggles.

"What does that mean?" Rebecca says.

From all around them, a woman's voice booms, "Aly, that's no way to behave. She really doesn't know why she's here."

Rebecca looks around. "Hello? Who are you? Where are you?" She gets no response. The words sink in. "Aly?" She looks again to the blonde girl. "Alyssa? You're Alyssa Walker? I know you, but not as a kid."

"I am who I am, that's all that I am," Alyssa says, almost singing the words. "Sorry. I like riddles. Mama always tells me to speak plainly. Riddles are fun, though."

The door opens and a black man, around thirty and not dressed like a hospital employee, enters. "Aly, the nurse said you're awake. Thank god."

"Maybe this guy can tell me something," Rebecca says.

Alyssa tumbles sideways off the bed and crouches beside it, watching the action with a gleam in her eye, as the man goes to Rebecca and gives her an emotional hug. Rebecca is caught off guard and pushes him away.

"What's wrong, Aly?" the man says.

"First, that's not my name and second, who the hell are you?" Rebecca says. She glances at Alyssa who seems amused by the exchange.

"Aly, I'm Tim — your husband," he says.

"Stop calling me that!" Rebecca says. "My name is Rebecca Asher and I've never seen you before in my life."

"We've been married for over a year," the man says.

"Oh, we have, have we?" Rebecca says. "I have a fairly good memory of what I was doing throughout twenty-o-four and getting married to you isn't on the list."

"We were married August 18, two thousand nine," Tim says.

"Twenty-o-nine?" Rebecca says. "Nice try, Future Boy. Did you come here in your DeLorean? This is November twenty-o-five. I'm not stupid."

"No, this is August two thousand ten," Tim says. "We were supposed to go out to celebrate our first anniversary the day you were in the accident."

"Twenty-ten? Talk about your Big Sleep." Rebecca focuses on Alyssa again. "Do you know this guy, Aly?"

"Maybe — someday," Alyssa says with a giggle.

"Who are you talking to?" Tim says.

"What do you mean, who am I talking—" Rebecca breaks off and looks at Alyssa, then back to Tim. A realization hits her. "How many people do you see here? In the room. Other than you."

Tim looks around, confused. "Just you."

"Oh," Rebecca says. She considers this. "When you look at me, are you seeing a really short woman with frizzy black hair, or a tall blonde?"

Tim gives her another curious look and surveys the room again. "Is this a joke?"

"No," Rebecca says. She glances down at Alyssa. "Definitely not a joke."

"I see you — Alyssa — a tall blonde," Tim says. "Wait." He checks the room. Barely under his breath, he says, "No mirrors." Spying Alyssa's bag on the credenza, he holds up a finger, then retrieves the bag. Rummaging around, he finds a little mirror and hands it to Rebecca. She hesitates, then raises the mirror. Looking back at her is an older version of the young girl crouched beside the bed. Seeing this, the girl pops up, clapping her hands, and chanting, "You are me as I am you!"

Rebecca lowers the mirror and shakes her head. Looking toward the ceiling, she says, "Now would be a good time for another one of those announcements."

Tim follows her gaze, but still can't see anyone or anything out of the ordinary in the room. "The doctor said there might be some complications from the accident. How are you feeling?"

Rebecca places a hand to her head. "I feel like the Braves hitting roster has been using my head for batting practice." Tim starts to respond but Rebecca puts up her hands. "Forget that, Future Boy. Can you tell me if my brother Steven is around somewhere? I really need to see him."

"Protect the boy!" Alyssa proclaims. "That's why we're here."

"You don't have a brother," Tim says.

"Oh, give me a damn break," Rebecca replies. "He's the only family I have left after our mom died. That's not counting the dead-beat dad who walked out on us when I was a kid."

"You don't have a brother," Tim insists. "You have an older sister — Leah. She's very worried about you. We've both been. Your mother died when you were a kid and you were raised by your father who was one of the finest men I've ever met."

Rebecca looks quickly in Alyssa's direction, then says, "I have no idea what is going on here. The last thing I remember I was headed away from Braselton. Maybe I collided with a truck?"

The woman's voice booms again from all around the room.

"An Atlanta woman was killed Tuesday in a head-on collision outside Braselton."

Tim shakes his head. "You weren't anywhere near Braselton. You crashed into a wall on Peachtree Parkway while you were headed home. The police said you swerved to avoid another accident and lost control of the minivan."

"I have never driven a minivan," Rebecca says, "and there's no reason whatsoever for me to be on Peachtree Parkway — wherever the hell that is."

"It's near John's Creek," Tim says.

"Why would I be headed to a creek?" Rebecca asks. "I live in East Lake."

"No, we live in John's Creek," Tim says.

"Not a creek, Future Boy — East Lake," Rebecca says. "My family's owned that house since I was in grade school. It's probably the only thing my father ever got right considering the place is worth a fortune since the area's been gentrified."

A distinguished older man dressed like a doctor enters, followed by the nurse. Rebecca waves her hand toward them. "Oh, look, Lana's back. I guess that makes you Dr. Kildare."

The doctor speaks. "Dr. Gardner actually. How are you feeling?"

Rebecca leans toward him and speaks harshly. "I woke up to find Snapshot McCall hovering over me then Marty McFly comes in telling me I'm his wife. How do you think I feel?"

The doctor examines Rebecca. "Let's take a look." Alyssa climbs onto the bed again to get a better vantage point.

Tim goes to the nurse. "Lana, are there any Internet terminals on this floor?"

She shakes her head. "Sorry, no public terminals in the hospital."

He takes out his phone. "No problem." He dials and heads toward the door. "Leah, it's Tim. Did I wake you? Good. Listen, Aly's awake, but she's acting really weird. Right, but before that, I need you to look something up on the Internet."

Alyssa lingers outside a clothing store at Lenox Mall, staring at a dress in the shop window, trying to convince herself it's something she'd buy. It's late-May of 2005, and Alyssa has been out of college for more than six months. She had been accepted for graduate school in Connecticut but yielded to her father's recommendation that she remain closer to home. He'd always been there for her following her mother's death, and she felt a bit guilty being so far away from him.

Her thoughts are interrupted by a familiar voice that comes from over her shoulder. "Aly?"

Alyssa turns to see Rebecca Asher standing there, holding a shopping bag. "Becky!"

They hug one another enthusiastically.

"I have not seen you in forever!" Rebecca says. Alyssa notes that Rebecca's manner of speaking is different than she recalls, and it sounds like she's imitating someone famous, but Alyssa can't place who it is. "I tried calling you a few times after I got back from Florida, but never heard back from you."

"I tried calling you, but the number you gave me was disconnected," Alyssa says.

"Disconnected?" Rebecca says. "My number's never been disconnected. No matter, we're here now. How've you been?"

"Great," Alyssa says. "I finished college last year and decided to take some time off before grad school. I've got a job nearby and have lunch here all the time."

Rebecca holds up the bag from a men's store, "I'm shopping for a graduation present for my little bro."

"Steven, right?" Alyssa says.

"You remember," Rebecca says.

"Oh, I remember everything." Alyssa taps her head. "I'm like the Georgia Archives."

"Are they expecting you back at work?" Rebecca asks.

"No," Alyssa says. "The office was dead, so they said I could start the weekend early."

"Let's hang out!" Rebecca says.

"I would love that," Alyssa says. "So, what have you been up to? Are you married?"

"Ah, no," Rebecca says. "Girls like me can't get married in Georgia."

Alyssa gets it. "I never realized."

"Back then I wasn't so sure myself," Rebecca says. "But we've got all afternoon to talk about that. Say, you like movies? Old movies, like the forties and fifties."

"Sure," Alyssa says.

"Then I am treating you to the Rebecca Asher inaugural film festival in East Lake."

Rebecca is lying on the bed with Alyssa wandering around the room, exploring.

"I don't like hospitals," Alyssa says. "Mama went to one and never came back. Besides, we should be protecting the boy."

This causes Rebecca to remember her brother, Steven. She retrieves the phone and dials a number. It takes a couple of rings before a man picks up and says, "This is Steve."

"Stevie!" Rebecca says. "Oh — my — god it is so good to hear your voice. You won't believe the day I'm having. Listen, I'm prepared to forgive you for not being here when I woke up if you'll just come down here and get me the hell out of this nut house."

There's a long pause before the man responds. "Who's this?"

"What do you mean, who's this?" she says. "It's Becky — your sister."

"Okay, that's not funny," Steven says, a note of anger in his voice. "Who is this?"

Rebecca is confused but takes stock of herself and realizes the problem. "Oh, Christ. I don't sound like myself, do I? Trust me, Goonie. It's Becky."

"What did you—?" He stops. "Do not call me that. Nobody calls me that anymore."

"I've been calling you that since you were eight," she says. Dial tone.

Rebecca redials. The phone rings several times before Steven picks up.

"Stevie?" Rebecca says.

"Look, I don't know who you are or what kind of sick game you're playing but Becky is dead," he tells her. "Now stop calling me." He hangs up.

Rebecca sits, with the phone in her lap. The last pronouncement by the Voice echoes again in her head. "An Atlanta woman was killed in a car accident outside Braselton."

She picks up the phone and dials once again and doesn't wait for Steven to say anything. "Don't hang up! Just listen to me. Go upstairs to my—" She shakes her head. "To Rebecca's room. In the closet, near the back, is a loose floor board. You'll find a lockbox there. If you haven't rearranged things, the key is taped to the back of the mirror."

"What are you talking about?" Steven says.

"Just do it," she says. "You'll be really surprised by what you find there. We can talk about it when I see you." She hangs up without awaiting a response.

"Aly, what would you say to a road trip?" Rebecca says.

"Florida?" Alyssa says.

"No, East Lake," Rebecca says.

"A quest!" Alyssa says. "To protect the boy."

"I'm not sure he's the one who going to need protecting, but if that's how you want to see it, fine," Rebecca says.

Rebecca goes to the credenza, where some clothes are neatly folded. When she holds up the jeans, they're almost as long as her entire body. You've got to be kidding. The clothes all seem to fit, though. She touches her head and feels a bandage. *Better leave that.* Tim's baseball cap is hanging on a chair. Rebecca picks it up and tries it on. *Too big.* She makes an adjustment, and it fits. She picks up the zippered bag and looks around. Alyssa is seated on the credenza. Rebecca says, "You coming?"

"I'll meet you there," Alyssa says, then vanishes.

Rebecca opens the door, not certain how much opportunity she'll have to make her getaway. She looks out and sees several nurses gathered at the station, halfway down the hall, with the elevator on the other side. Before she has time to formulate a plan, some people come out of a nearby room and walk past, so she falls in with them, easily getting past the station where the nurses are talking. At the opposite end of the hall, Rebecca spots the woman who identifies herself as Alyssa's sister, Leah, talking to one of the nurses. She lowers her head and boards the elevator with the group. On the ground floor, Rebecca exits the elevator, but hesitates when she sees police officers. *Don't stop unless they stop you.* She walks toward the automatic doors and feels a cool breeze as she exits. Then the air gets hotter, heavier.

"August in Atlanta," Rebecca says to an officer who exits with her. He chuckles.

Alyssa is waiting for her at the Georgia State MARTA station. "Are we going to ride the train?"

"That's just what we're going to do, Aly," Rebecca says.

Rebecca goes to the ticket machine and gets one pass. Then she and Alyssa are on the platform. Then they're on the train. Then they're someplace called East Lake.

Tim boards the elevator on the main floor of Grady and presses the button for Alyssa's floor. He's happy she's awake but concerned about her personality change. He spoke to the doctor earlier but found the conversation less than reassuring.

"It's not just her memory, Doctor Gardner, her entire personality has changed," Tim said. "She's rude, sarcastic, and seems to have acquired a considerable interest in movie trivia."

"It's not unheard of for patients who've experienced this kind of trauma to undergo changes in personality," the doctor said.

"She won't even answer to her own name," Tim said. "She insists I call her Rebecca."

"There's a lot we don't understand about how the brain heals itself," Dr. Gardner said. "I can tell you the swelling has gone down, and the CT scan doesn't show any residual damage. Alyssa is a very lucky young woman. Things could have been much worse."

"My sister-in-law sent me details from an obituary she found online for a woman named Rebecca Asher who died in November two-thousand five, in a car accident outside Braselton," Tim said. "The obituary listed a brother Steven."

"Has Alyssa ever mentioned anyone by that name?" Dr. Gardner says.

"Not to me," Tim said. "We met in two-thousand eight, but her sister never heard of Rebecca Asher either."

"Even though we don't yet know the reason, there has to be one," the doctor says. "Until we figure that out, what Alyssa needs most is to be surrounded by the people she knows and loves."

Timothy Marcus Caine was born 10 October 1978 in Seattle, Washington, the middle son of Gerald and Naomi (Grant) Caine. A good student, he had a high aptitude for math and science, and maintained a B average throughout high school, where he played baseball and soccer, and was considered an above average player in each, though not quite talented enough for a scholarship in either. For college, he headed East to Atlanta during the Olympics, to attend Mercer, arriving early in the hopes of taking in some of the Games, getting here the day before the Olympic Park bombing. Eventually, he earned a bachelor's and master's degree in accounting, and took a job as a loan officer with a credit union, following graduation.

From an early age, Tim's parents instilled in him and his siblings a love for the outdoors, camping, hiking, and climbing, and once he'd settled into his job in Atlanta, he joined Natural Encounters, a singles group focused on outdoor activities. One morning, on an extended day hike to the North Georgia mountains, he found himself among a breakaway group of hikers which included an attractive blonde with a runner's physique who introduced herself as Aly, an elementary school teacher. As the hike progressed, Tim found himself engrossed in a conversation with her about education funding and how woefully inadequate she found the state's commitment to teaching, despite the funds coming in as a result of the lottery. As the subjects shifted, Tim noted Aly was laughing at his jokes, and asking him many questions, genuinely interested in getting to know him.

When they came to the end of the hike, Tim learned she was Alyssa Walker and that she lived on his side of town, near Lenox. He took a chance and asked if she'd be interested in meeting for coffee some afternoon and she proposed they have dinner instead.

Their first official date was to a sushi place on Buford Highway, and a movie at the metroplex on Interstate 85. From there they saw one another every few nights during the school year, and a few months after meeting one another, Alyssa took him home to meet her father. Working in the mortgage industry, Tim was familiar with Walker Development, and had heard of the role Paxton Walker played in shaping Atlanta, but the man Tim met seemed down to earth and welcoming, if a bit distant, and totally devoted to his youngest daughter. Tim did find it odd that, though Alyssa had mentioned having a sister, Leah, her name never came up throughout the evening. When he asked Alyssa about it afterward, she explained that Paxton and Leah weren't speaking to one another and it was good Tim hadn't brought it up while they were together. A few weeks later, Tim suggested Alyssa could move into his apartment, but she refused, not due to a lack of desire on her part, but because she wanted more of a commitment if they were going to live together. It took Tim another month or so, but finally he decided he'd found the woman with whom he wanted to spend the rest of his life and proposed. Alyssa joyously accepted.

The wedding was the most elaborate Tim had ever seen and he was glad his participation consisted of him showing up at the church on time, since he was certain the planning that went into this affair was a logistical nightmare. His extended family and friends took up most of the first three pews to the right of the altar, whereas Alyssa's family and friends, and her father's business associates, took up every available space left in the sanctuary that probably seated over three hundred. The wedding was presided over by a former mayor and United Nations Ambassador, and, at Alyssa's request, included the Rabbi from the Temple she attended as a child. Her immediate family took up the first few rows; important guests, of which there were quite a number, took up the next few. Tim was sure much of the wealth in Atlanta was in that sanctuary. Random friends took up the remaining seats. Alyssa had been upset to discover that a number of her father's family had refused to attend, but Tim learned after he arrived that another family member had interceded and gotten everyone there.

The ceremony itself rivaled a royal wedding in its opulence, the bride proceeded by a children's choir singing The Bride's Chorus from Lohengrin a cappella, followed by the flower girl, then the ring bearer, the bridal party, and, at last the bride and her father. They were followed by a woman with dark, reddish hair, distinctive blue eyes, and wearing a dark, man-tailored business suit, who nodded or otherwise acknowledged individuals in the bride's section. It was the first time Tim had actually seen Alyssa's sister, who Paxton had tried to exclude from the guest list. As Paxton and Alyssa stopped at the altar, Leah slipped behind them and took a seat in the front pew. The ceremony itself was short and to the point. Tim and Alyssa had prepared a few words, but otherwise, it was a traditional ceremony. At the reception, Tim finally met Leah and got his first initiation into Walker family politics. Alyssa's mother's side of the family hardly interacted with anyone else in the family other than Leah, who seemed to go out of her way to avoid the wife of one of her uncles, and Paxton and Leah barely exchanged ten words between them.

In the months afterward, Alyssa slowly filled Tim in on the specifics of the tension between her father and sister as she knew them, and he began to notice how much influence Paxton had over Alyssa. She rarely contradicted anything her father said in front of him, and when Paxton would visit he often spoke to Alyssa like she was much younger and more immature than she actually is. Tim would watch his successful and competent wife revert to an awkward teenager in the presence of her father, constantly asking his advice, even on subjects in which she was well-versed, and withering whenever he'd make a negative observation about something she said or did. Her relationship with Paxton was the only reason Tim could fathom for Alyssa having very little contact with her sister, beyond phone calls and rare visits, and whenever he was over, Paxton would inquire if Alyssa had heard from Leah, and speak disapprovingly of Leah if Alyssa had. Tim learned, early on, that Paxton had offered considerable financial assistance to him and Alyssa, and he had to politely, but firmly refuse, which caused some tension with Alyssa, not because they needed the help, but because she didn't feel comfortable saying no to her father. Tim had gotten a sense of Alyssa's devotion to her father while they were dating, but it wasn't until they were together full-time that he realized the full extent of it.

Totally on his own, Tim rang up Leah while he was downtown once, and dropped by her office to get better acquainted. What struck him most about her was how much like Paxton she was, cordial but distant, revealing very little about how she felt about anything. He found her tendency to refer to Alyssa as "Princess" condescending, but had to admit it seemed to suit Alyssa, particularly when she was with her father. Leah had no blinders on about Paxton.

"He's offered you money, hasn't he?" Leah said when Tim inquired about Alyssa's past relationship with her father.

"Yes," Tim said.

"Typical," she said. "How did you respond?"

"When we were together, Alyssa and I agreed we didn't need it," Tim said. "But when he brought it up at the house, she said we hadn't made a decision. We actually got into an argument about it after he left."

"Yes, you'll see that pattern again," Leah said. "Alyssa was very young when Mom died, and Dad tends to be more than a little controlling."

"I've picked up on that," he said.

"If you really want to get into an argument, let her know you talked to me," Leah said.

"Then I shouldn't mention I saw you?" Tim says.

She leans forward. "Oh, you can mention it, just don't tell her what we talked about. Lay it on me. Tell her I set up the meeting and tried to pump you for info."

Tim nods.

"Step lightly when the subject of Dad comes up," Leah said. "It's Alyssa's major blind spot."

He had taken these words to heart and learned to navigate around interference from his father-in-law, occasionally having to assert himself, until he reached an uncomfortable truce. Paxton's death had thrown Alyssa into a deep sadness, and Tim has worried she might require professional help to work through it. He took it as a promising sign when she went back to her job, but now the car accident, followed by her personality shift has left him wondering how to help his wife.

He exits the elevator and heads to Alyssa's room, finding it empty, and all her belongings missing. He hurries out and sees Leah and Nurse Turner talking at the other end of the hallway and moves swiftly toward them.

"Have either of you seen Alyssa?" he says.

"She was resting when I looked in on her," Nurse Turner says.

Leah nods. "Yeah, she looked like she was sleeping when I got here."

"She's not in her room and the clothes I brought for her are gone," Tim says.

"I'll alert security and let the doctor know," Nurse Turner says as she moves away from them.

"Does she have your car keys?" Leah says.

"No, but she has her bag with her money and credit cards," he says. "Say, where is East Lake from here?"

"It's near my old place in Kirkwood," Leah says.

"Can you give me directions?" Tim says. "I think I know where she went."

"Sure." Leah takes out a notepad and pen. "Want me to tag along?"

"It's probably best if I go alone," he replies. "She's pretty much reacted the same toward both of us, but if she's where I think she's gone, I don't want to overwhelm the person there."

As Leah writes, she says, "That address I gave you is actually in Oakhurst. I flipped some property there once. You'd think East Lake Drive would be in East Lake, but it's not."

"Whatever it's called, that's probably where she is," he says.

Leah hands him the directions. "Call me if you need me. Good luck."

Goonie

Steven moves anxiously around the room, still reeling from the phone call he received from the mysterious woman. He found the lockbox and key in the places she said they were and the box was full of cards and letters sent to Rebecca from their father, Owen, which she kept for some reason. He wonders how the woman on the phone knew they were there, and, more ominously, what she meant when she said she'd see him. *Did Claire get a call?* He grabs the portable phone, sits on the couch, and dials a number. A woman answers. "Hey Steven. I was just thinking about calling you. What are you up to a week from Friday?"

"I don't think I'm doing anything," he says. "What's up?"

"I'm taking an improv class at the Comedy Factory and Friday's my graduation performance," she says.

"I'll try to make it," he says. "Listen, I had a strange call from some woman claiming to be Becky."

"Are you serious?" she says. "That sounds freaky. Did you recognize her voice?"

"It didn't sound like Becky, but her voice did sound familiar," he says. "She also knew some things only Becky would know. I wanted to give you a heads up in case she tries to contact you."

"Thanks for the warning," Claire says. "That would really ruin my day."

He's interrupted when the doorbell rings several times quickly, and someone starts pounding on the door.

"What's that?" Claire asks.

"I think this might be round two," he says. "I need to go check before whoever this is beats the door down."

"Maybe you should just call the cops," Claire says.

"You're probably right," he says. "Hopefully, I'll talk to you soon."

"Be careful," she says.

He concludes the call and goes to the window overlooking the porch. Outside is a tall, slender, blonde woman in jeans and a plaid top who's wearing what appears to be a Seattle Mariners baseball cap. She's watching the window and when she sees him look out, she gestures to him, much in the way Rebecca sometimes did when she misplaced her keys and needed entry. Steven goes to the door and puts on the security latch, then opens the door. Before he can say anything, the woman says, "Find the letters?"

"Yes," Steven says. "How did you know they were there?"

"Guess there's only one way to find out," she says indicating the door.

"Are you here alone?" Steven says.

The woman looks down and to her left. "For the most part."

Steven closes the door, removes the latch, and opens the door to admit the blonde woman. Once she's inside, he locks the door, and puts on the latch, then turns to her. "Start by telling me your name and how you know so much about my sister."

"Stevie it's me, Becky," the woman says, presenting herself to him. Ever since she returned from New York, Rebecca had affected a very distinctive way of speaking, emulating how Bette Davis spoke, and the woman addresses him this way, though how she does it sounds contrived. "I woke up at Grady this morning, in this body, and attached to a ten-year-old Mini-Me that no one else seems to know is there."

"Okay," Steven says, backing away from her and toward the phone. "Grady, eh? I think I'm just going to ring up the authorities to let them sort this out."

The woman goes to him. "I know this sounds crazy. How do you think I feel?" An idea comes to her. "Listen to me. You are Steven Charles Asher. Born March 3, 1987. Mother, Sharon Elizabeth Asher, born May 31, 1959, died from ovarian cancer June 16, 1997. Father, Owen Monroe Asher, a pilot with Northwest, who ditched out on his family when you were three. Ring a bell?"

"Very impressive," he says, "but every bit of that is readily available online. It doesn't prove a damn thing."

The woman gets a bit choked up as she says, "Okay, how about this? On the night our mother died, you asked me why I wasn't crying. I told you it was because I had to be strong for both of us. Remember? You said it was okay. You'd be sad for both of us."

For a long moment he cannot speak. When he again finds his voice, he moves slowly toward her. "Who are you and how do you know that? No one else was in the chapel at the time Becky and I had that conversation."

The woman touches his shoulder. "Your sister was there."

Steven sighs then goes to the credenza and grabs a photo of Rebecca. He takes it to her. "This is Becky."

The woman takes the photo, looks it over, then back to Steven. As she speaks, her eyes dart around the room as though she's tracking someone. "I know that's how I should look. Mind you, I'm not complaining because I think I look pretty hot in this bod." She looks toward the couch and says, "No, no. Get down from there, Sweetie."

Steven looks and sees no one. "Who do you see there?"

"Me," she says. She waves her hand in front of herself. "Or rather, her."

"Her, who?" Steven says.

"Alyssa," she says.

"Alyssa?" Steven says. "Alyssa Caine?"

She nods. "Walker to me, but yeah, I think it's Caine now. Does that mean something to you?"

Steven puts his hand against his face and turns away from her. "Yeah, as a matter of fact, it does. Now I know where I've heard your voice."

A young woman with a guitar, who introduced herself as Amy, is seated on a barstool singing to a sparse crowd of listeners, as Alyssa sips her coffee. Across from her, Rebecca is sitting sideways in her chair, enrapt by the song. They had been chatting about their respective trips to Florida for Spring Break, but once Amy started her set, Rebecca insisted they pay attention, and not be like the other patrons, who are contributing to the low din that hovers around the room and not really listening to the performer. Alyssa uses the opportunity to take stock of her new acquaintance.

Rebecca has an animated personality and is obviously well-read on a variety of subjects. Her passions seem to be music and movies — when Alyssa brought up the last two films she'd seen, Rebecca praised the dark humor of Rushmore and said she thought Shakespeare in Love was okay, though she's usually not a fan of "costume dramas" or "sappy" love stories. She also mentioned she is on a list that receives passes to preview movies before they premiere in theaters. Her sense of humor reminds Alyssa of kids at her school who watch Monty Python and play fantasy role-playing games on Nintendo or PlayStation, and when speaking, Rebecca races from topic to topic, as ideas occur to her. From almost the moment they met, Rebecca has seemed in charge, like she's guiding their plans or which topics to discuss. Though they look nothing alike, a lot of how Rebecca presents herself puts Alyssa in mind of her sister, Leah, from when Alyssa was smaller. Perhaps that's why she's felt comfortable around Rebecca from the start. She worries, though, how Sandy and Mandy will react to her, because Alyssa wants her to join them while they're in Florida.

Amy finishes her set and, after packing up her guitar, heads to the table with CDs and other merchandise. Rebecca turns back toward Alyssa and collapses into her seat. "Oh — my — god. She has the voice of an angel. I want to get a CD."

"So, let's do it," Alyssa says. "I'll get us both one."

"Look, I do have some money," Rebecca says.

"Becky, stop worrying about it," Alyssa says, leaning toward her and touching her hand. "You saved me, remember?" She grabs her purse and shakes it.

"Oh, yeah, I did, didn't I?" Rebecca says.

They head over to the merchandise table where they chat with Amy and Alyssa buys two copies of the three albums she has for sale.

"You just financed my road trip to Austin," Amy says.

Alyssa looks at the cover of one of the CDs and notes a different name. She says, "Shayna?"

Amy tells her, "It's the name I perform under when I go electric."

Rebecca signs up for the mailing list and praises Amy's singing, mentioning other singers who match her style, which impresses Amy. Alyssa doesn't recognize the names. Learning she'll be in Atlanta in a few weeks, Rebecca says to Alyssa, "We should go to the show."

Back at their table, Rebecca says, "So, tell me about these other girls you're with."

"They're my best friends," Alyssa says. "I've known Sandy since I moved to Lawrenceville and Mandy since third grade."

"I have a couple friends like that," Rebecca says. "They're probably whooping it up in Orlando right now."

"I can't believe you drove down here all by yourself," Alyssa says. "Weren't you bored?"

"Not really," Rebecca says. "I was more afraid my car would crap out. It's a good car but has nearly three hundred thousand miles on it."

They chat for several minutes before the emcee announces that the next performer will begin in five minutes. A young man with a guitar and harmonica begins tuning up. Rebecca swirls the coffee around in her cup, then finishes it off. Indicating Alyssa's cup, she says, "Need a refill, Andy?"

Alyssa gives her an odd look, not sure she heard what she thinks she heard. "Excuse me?"

Rebecca seems to catch herself, looks down, hesitates, then smiles and points to Alyssa's cup. "Your coffee? Aly? Need a refill?"

Alyssa looks over Rebecca a moment, then at her cup, and

shakes her head with a smile, convinced she misheard. "Oh. No. I'm fine."

Rebecca puts her bag over her shoulder. "So, let's go find your friends."

Using Leah's directions and the info she sent him on Rebecca Asher earlier, Tim finds his way to East Lake Drive. He parks in front of the house at 466, a two-story unit that looks like it was built mid-century. At the door, a tall man with dark hair, who appears to be in his twenties, answers, behind a security latch.

"Can I help you?" he says.

"Are you Steven Asher?" Tim asks.

"Yes," he says.

"Hi, I'm Tim Caine. I'm hoping you might know where my wife Alyssa is."

Steven sighs and nods then opens the door for Tim. "In here." Alyssa is standing near the couch, looking as though she's watching someone who's seated.

"Alyssa!" Tim says. "Thank god. You had us worried sick."

Alyssa looks in his direction and says, "Oh great. It's Marty McFly. How did he find us?" She reacts to something and looks at the couch. "Breadcrumbs?"

"Can you tell me what's going on here, Mr. Caine?" Steven says. "Your wife hasn't been much help."

"Please, call me Tim," he says.

"My sister's death was very tough on me, Tim," Steven says. "Your wife obviously knows a lot about Becky, but so far, aside from claiming to be her, she hasn't told me anything useful."

"Alyssa was in a very serious car accident a few days ago," Tim says. "She was in a coma until this morning and when she came out of it, she claimed she was Rebecca Asher and asked for you."

"I see," Steven says. "Well, I just found out she's Alyssa Caine." Steven goes to his answering machine. "There's something you both need to hear." Steven plays Alyssa's message, and the machine gives the date and time of the call.

"That's almost to the minute when Alyssa was in the accident," Tim says. "Here's something for you to ponder." He approaches Alyssa. "Rebecca, why don't you tell Steven the date you thought it was when you woke up?"

"November 29th, twenty-o-five," Alyssa says.

"November 29th?" Steven says. "That's the date—"

"Yeah, I saw her obituary on the Internet," Tim says. "Did Rebecca ever mention Alyssa Walker to you?"

"Not that I recall," Steven says. "Becky had a relatively small circle of friends, but I admit I didn't know them all."

"Will you please stop talking about me like I'm not here?" Alyssa says. "The last thing I remember, I was coming back from a perfectly horrible film festival in South Carolina."

"Becky's a film buff who did cultural items for Creative Loafing and several online sites," Steven says.

"Yeah, she's been quoting movies since she woke up," Tim replies.

Alyssa sits and says, "The festival was beyond dreadful. I don't know what inspires these tiny bergs with an old movie house to think they can be the next Sundance."

This catches Steven's attention. He moves toward Alyssa. "What you just said. I've heard it before."

"Yeah, like five seconds ago," she says. "I just said it."

Steven shakes his head. "No, before that." He goes to his computer and does a search. "Here it is." He reads. "I don't know what inspires these tiny bergs with an old movie house to think they can be the next Sundance."

"What are you reading?" Tim says as he walks toward Steven.

Steven looks toward Tim. "Becky's story about the festival. It's the last thing she ever published." He looks at Alyssa. "You quoted it word for word."

"So? I wrote it," she says.

Tim says, "Aly mentioned something about Braselton. I noted that's where Rebecca was killed."

Steven nods. "Just outside Braselton, an eighteen-wheeler crossed the center line and plowed into Becky's car at about sixty miles an hour. The report said the driver fell asleep. Becky drove a Mini Cooper so there wasn't much left of it."

Tim nods. "I saw the write up on the accident. Pretty horrific."

"The paramedics were pretty sure she died on impact," Steven says. "After seeing what was left of her I hoped they were right. We couldn't have an open casket at the funeral."

"That must have been terrible," Tim says.

"It was the toughest thing I've ever had to do in my life," Steven replies. "I hate that it's the last image I'll ever have of her."

"I apologize if we're adding to your troubles," Tim says. "We weren't expecting this turn of events either."

He begins filling Steven in on the background of how they came to be here. While he does, Alyssa sits on the couch, looking to her left, as though she's listening to someone else.

Alyssa walks with Rebecca out to the parking lot at Lenox Mall, where they climb into Rebecca's copper-colored Mini Cooper. "Quite an upgrade from what you were driving before."

"Yeah. I'm a big Jason Bourne fan," Rebecca says. As they pull out onto Lenox Road, she says, "Connector shouldn't be too bad this time of day."

"It's a holiday weekend. People may leave early."

"Good point," Rebecca replies. "But, we'll take our chances."

Once they're on the freeway, Alyssa says, "I'm sorry we lost touch after Florida."

"Yeah. I tried calling and your father quizzed me on who I was and how I knew you, then said he'd have you call me," Rebecca says. "I never heard anything."

"I got your messages, but you never left a number," Alyssa says. "The number you gave me in Florida was disconnected."

"My home number's the same as it's always been," Rebecca says. "It's never been disconnected." She takes a card from her pocket and hands it to Alyssa. "See?"

Alyssa looks at the number. "One, four, eight, five? You gave me one, four, five, eight."

"Oh," Rebecca says. "Sometimes I mix up numbers when I'm writing them down. Sorry about that."

"I tried looking you up, but your number was unlisted," Alyssa says.

"My aunt changed the number and had it unlisted after my Mom died to keep my father from contacting us," Rebecca says.

"I remember you talking about that," Alyssa says. "How'd it all work out?"

"We'll have to save that discussion for when we're at the house," Rebecca says. "Not a simple story at all."

They make it through Atlanta traffic just as it's starting to get heavy and reach Oakhurst in a little over forty-five minutes. Once there, Rebecca opens a bottle of wine and pours them each a glass, which they sip as they catch up on what they've been doing since Florida. Finally, Rebecca goes to choose some titles for them to watch. On the way over, Alyssa mentioned several movies she's always wanted to see, and Rebecca agreed to play them, if she still has them. In addition, Rebecca pulls a few obscure titles before settling on three to start their film viewing.

"What have you got there?" Alyssa says when Rebecca returns with her selections. Rebecca holds up the titles as she says, "All About Eve — as you requested. Also, Key Largo." She pauses on the final one. "And one you probably never heard of, Homecoming."

"Sounds pleasant," Alyssa says.

"It's a World War II flick with Lana Turner and Clark Gable," Rebecca explains.

"Hey, Rhett Butler," Alyssa says.

"Right, but this is the post-war Gable," Rebecca says. "After he lost Carol Lombard. It's a bit obscure, but this will be perfect to start our little film fest." Rebecca puts the DVD in and sets the others on the machine. "Sit back and grab your handkerchief. The remote is on the table beside you. I'll go fix some popcorn." She starts toward the kitchen, then turns back. "How are doing on wine?"

Alyssa lifts the bottle. "We're good."

Rebecca ponders it. "I'll break out another one just in case."

In Homecoming, which Rebecca plays first, Clark Gable is Dr. Ulysses Johnson — with obvious allusions to Homer's Ulysses — a surgeon who joins the Army, where he meets Jane "Snapshot" McCall, an Army nurse played by Lana Turner, with whom he falls in love. Prior to enlisting, he is cold and callous toward his patients, but experiences during his service cause him to reevaluate how he treats those who seek his care. At the close of the war, he returns home to his wife, a changed man.

Alyssa dries her eyes constantly throughout the end of the film, just as Rebecca said she would.

Just after the movie, Rebecca says she has to do something in the kitchen, and heads in. Alyssa takes the opportunity to explore the house. She wanders over to a console table near the front door that's laden with family photos and she lifts a couple and examines them. As she's doing so, someone rings the doorbell, then begins pounding on the door. Alyssa steps over to the window overlooking the porch and discovers Rebecca standing there, staring over at the window. When she sees Alyssa peer out, she gestures to the door, and Alyssa goes and opens it.

"Thanks," Rebecca says as she enters. "I went out for a smoke break and locked myself out." She goes into the kitchen and retrieves her keys.

"Why didn't you just knock on that door?" Alyssa says.

"There's a little vestibule leading to the back door, so it's easier to hear me from the front," Rebecca says. "No biggie. Want to watch Eve?"

"Sure," Alyssa says.

"And don't worry about the time, because we are having a sleepover," Rebecca says.

"Great," Alyssa says. "At some point, I need to call Daddy, so he doesn't get worried when I'm not at home."

"You live with your Dad?" Rebecca says.

"No, he just likes for me to be home when he calls," Alyssa says. "Otherwise, he gets worried and thinks I've been kidnapped."

"I can't imagine having a father like that," Rebecca says.

"I'm sure your father cares more than you think," Alyssa says.

"He has a lousy way of showing it," Rebecca replies.

"Some people are just like that."

"Yeah, and some people just run out on the people who need them," Rebecca says.

Alyssa shakes her head. "So, you're just going to hate your father for the rest of your life?"

"For your information. I don't hate my father. I'm mad as hell at my father and may be for the rest of my life but I don't hate him. He tried to contact me after my mother died. Said he wanted to make up for all the time we'd missed."

"Did you believe him?"

"Not for a second," Rebecca says. "He thinks he can ditch out on his responsibilities then just waltz back in and resume playing Daddy. He called. He sent letters. Then one day he just showed up at my dorm. Junior year. I told him to hop back into his damn plane and fly the hell out of there. He still sends an occasional letter or card."

"Which I suppose you burn," Alyssa says.

"Actually, I keep them stored away in a lock box hidden in my closet," she says. "I'll show them to you if you really want to see."

"If you want," Alyssa says, then runs her hand over Rebecca's shoulder. "You could try forgiving him, you know."

Rebecca shakes her head. "He needs to feel what it's like to not know if he'll ever see me again — the way I've felt. When I feel he's learned his lesson, then maybe we can talk." She starts toward the stairs. "Come on. This won't take long."

Rebecca has been staring at the table with photos. She rises and goes over with Alyssa following her. Rebecca picks up a photo of her and Steven as children with a woman who has strawberry blonde hair. "Mom."

Steven walks over and looks at the photo. "That's right."

"God, I miss her." Rebecca puts down the photo and picks up one of a young man in a leisure suit, who looks like he could be Steven's older brother. "Who's this guy?"

Steven seems surprised by the question. "You don't recognize him?"

"No, but something tells me I don't like him," Rebecca says.

Steven takes the photo and holds it so Tim can see it. "This is my father. Becky's father."

This catches Alyssa's attention. "Owen the pilot!"

Rebecca seems stunned. "This is Owen the pilot?"

Alyssa mimics an airplane. "Flew right out of our lives."

Steven speaks to Tim. "Becky would have recognized this photo. It was hers, but after Mom died, she threw it in the trash. I took it out and hid it in my room."

Steven turns back to Rebecca. "Let me ask you something — Rebecca. Why do you keep calling me 'Goonie?'"

"It's from the movie," she says. "We watched it as kids."

"True, but why specifically do you call me that?" he presses.

Rebecca considers the question. Suddenly, Alyssa says, "I know this." She runs to Rebecca. "When Stevie was eight—" She closes her eyes and concentrates like a small child would.

Rebecca meets Steven's eyes as the words come to her. "When you were eight, for some reason, you started insisting everyone call you 'Chuck'. I thought it was stupid, so I started calling you 'Chunk' like the kid in the movie. Mom got on my case about it, so I switched to 'Goonie' instead."

Steven stares at her. "Unbelievable."

Tim says, "Is that right?"

"That's how I remember it," Steven says.

Alyssa seems deep in thought. "Ask about the fair maiden."

Rebecca becomes anxious. "Forget that, Goonie. How is Claire?"

"You know Claire?" Steven says.

Alyssa claps her hands. "Clarabella!"

"Of course, I remember my Clarabella," Rebecca says. "Is she okay?"

"Yeah, she's fine," Steven says. "I just talked to her."

"Who's Claire?" Tim asks.

"She's the love of my life, Future Boy," Rebecca says. "See, that's why you and I can't be married. Girls like me can't get married in Georgia." She considers it. "At least I guess we still can't."

Steven shakes his head and says, "Love of your life?" He starts to go on but stops. Instead, he asks her, "What do you remember about Claire?"

"Very high maintenance," Rebecca says "hell, we both are — but worth the trouble. I mean, she can be quite a handful sometimes, but she cares for me like no one else."

"How does she look?" Steven says.

"Her looks?" Rebecca tries, but becomes frustrated. "Well, she's about — ah — okay, her hair is — dammit! Why can't I picture her?"

"You don't have any photos of the love of your life!" Alyssa says bouncing up and down.

"I didn't think you'd be able to," Steven says. "You've never seen her."

"We've been going out for a year and a half," Rebecca says. "It's kind of hard not to see someone under those circumstances."

Tim catches on. "Alyssa never saw her. Rebecca doesn't have any pictures?"

"Claire's very flaky about having her picture taken," Steven says. "I don't think I've ever seen one of her as an adult."

Tim indicates Rebecca. "I think I get this. Alyssa knew Rebecca, and I'll bet you dollars to doughnuts Alyssa's been to your house. She's seen your mother's photo but not your father's and she been told about Claire but never met her."

Alyssa claps her hands, bouncing up and down. "Ding, ding, ding, ding! Ten points for Timmy!"

"Okay, obviously, she doesn't have all Becky's memories, but what she does know is frightening," Steven says, mostly to Tim. "Could she remember all those details?"

"Oh yeah. Alyssa would remember," Tim says.

"Like the Georgia Archives," Alyssa says. She snaps her fingers and suddenly she and Rebecca are alone in the room.

"What just happened?" Rebecca says.

"We went back to the last time we were here," Alyssa says. She indicates the couch, where earlier versions of themselves are seated. "Although neither of us should remember very much from then." She waves her hand over the coffee table and several wine bottles appear.

Scenes unfold for Rebecca in quick succession of her and Alyssa in the living room, sometimes sitting on the couch staring at the television, sometimes moving around the room or leaving, separately or together. Throughout, they're drinking wine and having snacks. Eventually, they stop watching television and start dancing, then make a phone call before Alyssa passes out on the couch and Rebecca falls asleep in front of her laptop.

"Could we rewind that," Rebecca says. "I think I missed most of it."

"Don't worry, we'll see it all later," Alyssa says. She snaps her fingers again and they return to the room with Tim and Steven, who don't appear to have missed them.

"So, you have been here before," Rebecca says to Alyssa.
Tim looks at her. "What's that?"
"Nothing, never mind," Rebecca says.

The Ghost Queen

It is late-summer, 1965, and Sarah Rosales is going to Atlanta. She's eighteen, recently graduated high school, and on a Greyhound bus to Agnes Scott College in the suburbs of town, where she's enrolled as a freshman. Sarah, average height and medium build, with dark auburn hair and hazel eyes, is the second of four daughters of Benjamin and Esther Rosales of Charleston, South Carolina. She's the first of her family to live more than twenty miles from Charleston, and she's traveling to Atlanta to study and start her adult life. Her dream is to be a teacher, working with young children. She always got along well with her teachers and envied the influence they had on each successive class as they came and went. Now it's her turn to strike out and make a difference. The last thing for her to do, she thinks, as she's preparing for arrival, is to adopt her middle, secular name, so that when she sets foot in Atlanta for the first time, she'll be Melinda.

Once Melinda has gotten set up at school, she finds herself pulled into the sphere of influence of Margaret Blaine, an older and very formidable woman from Hancock County in Georgia, who's the daughter of Moreland Walker, owner of a chain of groceries throughout Georgia and the Carolinas. At age eighteen, against her family's wishes, Margaret married a produce salesman nearly-twice her age and came with him to Atlanta, where, five years into a hostile relationship, she divorced him and set out on her own. Now in her third year of studies at Agnes Scott, she's considered the Queen Bee, and is surrounded by numerous followers who imitate her clothing, speech, and mannerisms. One of Melinda's friends is a devotee of Margaret's and brings Melinda along to some outings, where Melinda fails to figure out what the fascination is with Margaret. Melinda's total lack of interest catches Margaret's attention and she sets out to learn more about this disinterested newcomer.

One afternoon, as Melinda is waiting for a cab to take her to Rich's downtown, Margaret appears and insists they share the ride. As soon as they're on their way, Margaret seems to want to chat, but Melinda is wary. Margaret is surprised to learn Melinda's a Jew and quizzes her about the religion. Against her better judgment, Melinda spends the entire afternoon with Margaret, who shows her all the places young, single women in Atlanta can enjoy themselves, with or without men present. By the time they return to campus, it's late, and just as Margaret predicted, Melinda now considers her a friend. Once she's friends with Margaret, Melinda's social life improves considerably, and her reputation among Margaret's crowd evolves from her being thought of as the quiet and studious Jewish girl to becoming the noisy life of the party with a dry wit, who doesn't suffer fools gladly.

Despite her late nights and occasional migraines, Melinda never misses a class nor fails to turn in an assignment on time, and still manages to keep up with her older compatriot, sometimes matching Margaret drink for drink, and turning away almost as many amorous suitors as her far more experienced friend. When Margaret's roommate graduates and moves back to Florida, Melinda gets first refusal on the room and moves in with Margaret. One afternoon, Margaret mentions that her younger brother, Lee, is moving to town to get a job and continue his education. Margaret invites Melinda to join them for dinner but explains that while his close family can still get away with calling him "Lee" to the rest of the world, he uses his middle name, Paxton.

Leroy Paxton Walker turns out to be very little like his older sister, a man of quiet intensity, thoughtful, and ambitious, who hates his first name as much as Margaret hates being called Peg. Between him and Margaret, Melinda learns Margaret is the only girl in the family, followed two years later by Paxton. Two other sons followed at three, then four-year intervals, Duane Willard, and Alexander Boyd. Paxton was expected to one day take over the family business, but instead studied architecture at UGA then headed to Atlanta to find an apartment and land a job with a development firm, while pursuing an advanced degree in civil engineering. His father still hasn't forgiven him. Paxton's goal is to one day start his own development firm. Melinda has a lovely time out with the brother and sister, and two days later is informed by Margaret that Paxton is quite taken with her. Melinda thinks nothing will come of it, due to their religious differences, and after two dates with Paxton, she lets him know that she doesn't wish to convert.

"I don't expect you to convert to a religion I hardly practice myself anymore," he responds to her relief.

While this reassures Melinda, she knows her family won't be happy. The more time she spends with Paxton, however, she begins to believe she could make a life with him. She decides to take the chance, and when her family comes to town for a visit, she introduces them to him. He hits it off with her father right away, and her sisters, Ruth, Debby, and Tamar, find him very attractive, but her mother says nothing, and betrays little of how she feels about this Gentile who's stolen her daughter's heart.

At last, as they're saying their goodbyes several days later, her mother proves to be her usual pragmatic self, stating, "If he lets you raise the children in Temple, what's the harm?"

Her mother and sisters head back to Atlanta to help plan the interfaith ceremony, scheduled to take place in June of 1968. Prior to the ceremony, Paxton receives a draft notice, which worries Melinda, but a congenital heart murmur prevents him from being called to serve.

After her marriage, Melinda continues attending classes at Agnes Scott, but as September wears on, she starts to feel a bit out of sorts and a visit to her doctor gives her the news that she's pregnant. She resolves to see the semester through, then conclude her college career, with an eye toward one day resuming it once her children are older. Paxton, certain their first child will be a boy, sets about putting together his own development firm, and schedules several meetings for late-May, but on May 23, the day he's meeting with investors, Melinda goes into labor, and Margaret drives her to Crawford Long Hospital. If it's a boy, the plan is to name him Moreland Benjamin, after his two grandfathers. A few hours later, however, Margaret manages to get a message to her brother that he's the father of a bouncing baby girl. Melinda names her daughter Leah, then Joanna, after Paxton's mother. Melinda knows she'll have to curtail her dreams of being a teacher, but no matter. *There will be time to teach other people's children,* she thinks, *now I must teach mine.*

This proves to be easy, for Leah is an inquisitive child with a fascination for science and how things work, and who picks up lessons quickly. Melinda tries to accommodate her daughter as much as possible, taking her to the High Museum, and Fernbank, and enrolling her in Pace Academy when she starts school. Leah is also very active, a bit of a tomboy, always out exploring, in shorts and oversized jerseys or rugby shirts, her favored attire, and only wears skirts to Temple or school, or whenever else Melinda makes her. Melinda takes a scattershot approach to educating Leah, buying her books on every topic, and enrolling her in extracurricular programs to supplement whatever she's learning in school. The family takes frequent trips to Europe, and Leah exhibits an aptitude for languages, quickly picking up most of the European dialects. The one aspect Melinda is not able to control, however, is Leah's relationship with her father. Paxton desperately wanted a son, and barely concealed his regret at the news he had a daughter. His business takes up much of his time, and it's painfully clear where his priorities lie when it comes to working or being with his family. When he is home, he's not much more attentive.

Melinda always sees so much hope in Leah's eyes when she tells her father about an accomplishment, and much disappointment when he dismisses her with a quick smile, or pat on the shoulder, or a half-hearted word of encouragement, before returning to his crossword, or putting practice, or any of the other, trivial activities he deems more important than spending time with his only child. Most of Leah's scorn, however, is directed at his company. Leah has taken to referring to the business as her father's favored child and resents every moment he spends with it instead of her. Margaret tries to fill the void, being the naughty aunt who lets Leah smoke around her — Melinda objects but can hardly criticize her daughter for a vice she herself practices — and giving Leah her first taste of wine before she's had her Bat Mitzvah or teaching Leah how to drive a stick shift in Margaret's Karmann Ghia. Yet, despite Leah's uneasy relationship with her father, each day, Melinda sees more of Paxton in how Leah interacts with people and studies any problem she encounters to find the best way to solve it.

He fails to see how much she truly is his daughter.

On the afternoon of 20 April 1981, with Margaret waiting at the family home to pick up Leah and give her the news, Paxton drives Melinda to Northside Hospital, where she delivers another healthy baby girl. For reasons known only to him, Paxton has chosen the name Alyssa, which no one in his family has, so Melinda honors the baby with her sister Ruth's name as well. Unlike Leah's birth, Paxton is there to witness this daughter's arrival, and Melinda can tell he's already invested in every aspect of Alyssa's life. This makes sense to Melinda. The thought comes to her:

I raised my husband's daughter, now he shall raise mine.

She's troubled by the implications of this thought, but lets it pass.

Melinda is pleased to see that Leah harbors no resentment for Alyssa, despite all the attention she receives from Paxton. In fact, Leah dotes on her sister almost as much as their father. Following her Bat Mitzvah, Leah takes on much more responsibility around the house, and looks for opportunities to spend time with her little sister, looking after her when Paxton and Melinda go out, becoming almost a second mother to Alyssa. Some years earlier, while Melinda's younger sister, Tamar, was visiting during a break in her first year of studies at the University of South Carolina, she revealed she was studying the Kabbalah. One evening, out of the blue, while she, Melinda and Leah were sitting on the front porch, Tamar predicted that Leah would one day have many children to bring her happiness in her old age, a suggestion to which Leah responded with very little enthusiasm. Secretly, however, Melinda takes Leah's new-found concern for Alyssa as an encouraging sign that Leah might one day make a good mother to her own children.

When the family moves to Lawrenceville, just prior to Alyssa starting school, Leah insists she be allowed to remain in the family's home in Buckhead, so she won't have a long commute to Pace for her senior year. Paxton and Melinda agree Leah's exhibited enough responsibility to be able to live on her own, and the independence she'll gain may serve her well when she goes away to college the following year. A few nights a week, Paxton also stays at the home when he needs to be at work early. While Melinda holds out hope this will bring Leah and her father closer together, Leah reports to Melinda when she's visiting Lawrenceville that this isn't the case.

The following year, after Leah drives off to Wellesley in Margaret's Karmann Ghia — a graduation present from her aunt — she manages to make it home for the holidays, but otherwise remains in Boston in an apartment she rents with another girl. When it comes time for Leah to graduate, Melinda happily anticipates watching her oldest daughter receive her diploma as Melinda had never done. As the graduation date nears, Melinda is aggravated when the migraines she experienced in college return with increased severity.

One evening, less than a week before Leah is to graduate, Melinda's in the kitchen, preparing supper when she starts to feel tension behind her eyes. She knows what that means, what it always means. Soon, she starts seeing wavy lines, and she feels slightly nauseous, the unmistakable harbinger of another migraine. This one feels more intense, more unrelenting, and she hopes she can head it off before it really takes hold. She lowers the heat on the pot she's stirring and goes into the living room, where Alyssa is sitting on the floor, watching one of her favorite television shows.

Melinda asks Alyssa to look after dinner, goes upstairs, takes three extra strength pain killers, and prepares herself a cold compress for her head. She lays on the bed and tries to get comfortable, but no matter how she lays, the pain and throbbing increases. Suddenly, she feels light-headed, and worries she'll be sick to her stomach, but then, the pain subsides completely, and she feels nothing. The light starts to fade, and darkness falls at the edge of her field of vision. She senses a presence in the room and looks to see Paxton, sitting on a chair near the bed, in his golf attire, with his head down. Without speaking, or acknowledging her, he dials a number, but she can't hear him — the scene seems like it's from a silent movie.

Paxton rises and goes to her. He leans in, kisses her, then places his hand over her eyes and closes them, and with that, she knows it's over. She feels the darkness close in on her, but she's not afraid. She left fear behind with her earthly remains. Instead, she waits to see what comes next. She does not know how long she's there, before a single thought comes to her, not a word, but a name, "Genevieve." In her mind, Melinda answers, "I accept." Then all goes dark. When she sees the light again, she will remember none of this.

Leah examines herself in the mirror as she parades around her bedroom wearing her cap and gown in Wellesley Blue, black, and cream. Seniors traditionally wear their graduation gowns on the last day of class, which was a few weeks ago, and Leah has worn hers, around the apartment at least, every day since, much to the amusement of her roommates Dottie and Dan. Commencement is less than a week away, and as her anticipation grows, Leah also looks forward to her future at MIT, where she's been accepted as an accelerated doctoral student. Throughout most of the year, she's been busy with her studies at both Wellesley and MIT, but as graduation nears, she's overcome with the sense she can accomplish anything. Her family is due late this week for the ceremony, and Leah especially can't wait to hug her mother and thank her for being her most consistent, tolerant, and loving teacher.

For most of her time at Wellesley, Leah has shared an apartment with a classmate, Dorothy Gage, who Leah knows as Dottie. Dottie is a wiry, energetic woman with curly, dirty-blonde hair and a endless supply of quips and biting commentary on the world around her. They met their freshman year, when Dottie showed up at Leah's dorm room, drunk, to confront Leah over an instructor who was a mutual love interest. Comparing notes, they realized they both were being lead on by the woman and contrived a means to put a stop to it and in the process became fast friends. The following summer they rented the apartment, which they quickly dubbed "Gomorrah East" and they have consistently tried to live up to the moniker with a steady stream of hookups coming in and out. On occasions throughout the time they've known one another their relationship has intensified, but they discovered they're happiest being good friends who enjoy spending time together.

Dan is a recent addition, who has been sleeping on the couch for several weeks, since his last roommate moved back to Toronto suddenly, leaving him with a place he couldn't afford on his own and unable to float the cost while he found someone new. In return for letting him crash there, he picks up the utilities. The trio met a little over a year ago at an improv club in Boston, near Wellesley's campus. Leah appreciates the fact that even though Dan has dated both she and Dottie, he never tries to worm his way into their beds. She was a bit wary of having two people in the house who knew her on such an intimate level, but the situation has proven beneficial for all three. Given their different schedules, there's usually someone home, and even though money has never been a problem for Leah, not having to pay the utilities is a welcome relief.

She hears the front door open and calls out, "Dottie?"

A man's voice comes back, "Dan."

She enters the living room and holds out her arms to model the gown for Dan, who shakes his head.

"Really? Leah?" he says. "I'm pretty sure they allow you to take the gown off when there are no official functions."

"Are you kidding? I sleep in it," she says. "They're going to have to cut it off me when I'm dead."

"You're not planning to wear it out tonight, I hope," he says, to which she shrugs. "I am so stoked about the show. There's supposed to be a group from Second City performing. I'm glad you're staying in the area, so we won't have to break up the act."

"Oh yeah, the act," Leah says. "Wouldn't want to deprive the world of Dander and Leander."

Dan shakes his head. "You're a better improviser than you think."

Leah puts her hands on her hips and tilts her head to the side. "Which explains why I'm always known as 'that chick who does improv with Dan'. You're the one who gets all the invitations to play with other groups."

"I take you along," he says. "I guess your folks are coming up for graduation?"

"The whole family," Leah replies. "Mom's supposed to call tonight to finalize details."

"As opposed to every other night when she just calls to chat," he says with a chuckle.

"So, I'm close to my mother, big deal."

"No, I think it's great. I wish I got along with my parents that well."

"Of course, they invite the controversial speaker the year before I graduate," Leah says. "We get a noted writer of young adult fiction."

"You're not a fan of Madeleine L'Engle?" he says.

"I enjoyed her books when I was a kid. Her writing is just a little below my grade level these days."

"How can you be a woman in science and not love A Wrinkle in Time?"

"I like it, okay?" Leah says. "It just made a larger impression on me when I was reading it at age eight than when I was reading it to my sister ten years later."

"Okay. I can understand that."

"Alyssa's the fantasy and make-believe enthusiast," Leah says. "I like my science down to Earth and hands-on."

The phone rings and Leah answers. "This is Leah. That you, Mom?" She's not expecting the voice on the other end of the line.

"No, Leah, it's me," Paxton says.

A tinge of fear runs through her. "Dad? Why are you calling? Where's Mom?"

Her father hesitates, then sighs. "Leah, your mother is dead."

Her stomach twists into a knot and her breathing quickens. She puts her hand to her head. "Wait. What did you just say?"

Leah exits into her room as Paxton repeats what he told her. "I'm sorry to be so blunt. I'm waiting for authorities."

"Where's Alyssa?" Leah says. "Does she know?"

"No. I sent her to Peg's," he says.

"You sent her to Margaret's before you called 911?" Leah says.

"What would you expect me to do?" he says. "I found Melinda upstairs. Alyssa was in the kitchen. This is— I'm sorry, Leah, someone's at the door. Please get here as quickly as you can." The line disconnects.

Leah circles around the room, still holding the phone, tears streaming down her cheeks, with her father's words echoing in her head. She stops, looks at herself in the mirror and the site of her graduation gown causes her to break into heavy sobs. She collapses onto the bed and buries her face into the pillow and lets out several sustained screams, beating the mattress with her fists. From what seems like a long distance away, she hears Dan call her name. Then someone pounds on the door and there's a different voice. It's Dottie. Leah pushes herself up from the bed and goes to the door. Dottie's just outside when she opens it and Leah falls into her arms, sobbing. Dottie comforts her.

"Dan said you were talking to your father. I knew something was wrong," Dottie says.

After a moment, Leah lifts her head. "He said my mother is—" She breaks off. "My mom's dead."

"Oh my god," Dan says.

Leah puts her hand to her head. "Dad didn't go into a lot of details. He came home and—" She wanders aimlessly away from them. "I've got to get to Atlanta. Tonight."

Dan says, "What can we do to help?"

"I need to—" Leah starts, then says, "What about graduation?"

Dottie takes her hands. "Don't worry about that now. You need to get home to your family."

Leah stares at her a moment and nods. "I'll need a flight out." She looks in the direction of her room. "I need to pack."

Dan takes the phone from Leah and says, "My cousin works for American Airlines at Logan. I'll call her and make the arrangements. If there's a direct flight out tonight, she'll get you on it." He starts to dial.

Dottie puts her arm around Leah and guides her into her room. "I'll help you get your stuff together. Let's get you home."

Leah and Alyssa sit on the couch in the living room at the Caine residence, looking through photos. Alyssa is dressed in shorts, sneakers and an Atlanta Braves jersey with the number ten.

"I hardly see what rummaging around in old photos is supposed to accomplish," Alyssa says in what sounds to Leah like a bad Bette Davis impersonation.

"You're trying to find yourself, Alyssa," Leah says. "Apparently, you've got to lose yourself to find yourself."

"Once again, I'm Rebecca," Alyssa says to Leah.

Leah is unimpressed. "Uh huh."

"Why is that so hard for you to believe?" Alyssa says.

Leah picks up her phone and displays a picture of Rebecca. "First, you don't look like her." She holds up a mirror. "You look like Alyssa."

"Okay, there's that," Alyssa says. "I can't explain that any more than you can."

"Second," Leah goes on, "you always run and hide when things get tough. Daddy can't protect you now, so instead you created your imaginary friend, Rebecca."

Alyssa glances to her left. "Really?"

Leah regards her with interest. "What was that?"

Alyssa looks back to Leah. "You're just a regular Anna Freud, aren't you? I bet spending the holidays with you is an absolute joy."

"I don't like dealing with middlemen," Leah says. "I need you to send the Princess out here, so I can talk to her."

Alyssa sighs. "What makes you think I can reach her?"

Leah points to Alyssa's head. "You exist in her head. Regardless of who you think you are, you are inhabiting the body of Alyssa Caine."

Alyssa glances to her left then says, "Let's say I agree with you. What am I supposed to do about that? As certain as you are that I'm Alyssa, I'm just as certain that I'm Rebecca."

"Okay, Rebecca," Leah says. "If you're a living breathing entity unto yourself, then let's get to know one another."

"Bring it on!" Alyssa says triumphantly. "No topic is off limits, girlfriend."

"Great," Leah says. "Tell me about your father."

Alyssa falls back onto the couch. "No topic except that one."

"What's the matter, Rebecca?" Leah says. "Surely you remember your Dad."

"The deadbeat who walked out on me when I was nine," Alyssa says.

"How about the doting Daddy who took early retirement to raise his little girl after his wife died?" Leah says. As an aside, she adds, "Probably the single most noble thing he ever did."

Alyssa won't look at Leah. "That's not my father."

"You sure about that?" Leah says. "From what Tim says, you couldn't identify the other guy."

"Did I mention I was nine when he left?" Alyssa says.

"You're telling me that in nine years you never looked at him?" Leah says. "Our father wasn't a huge presence in my life when I was a kid but at least I could pick him out of a photo line-up if I had to."

Alyssa gets angry and crosses her arms. "What's with the twenty questions? I thought we were supposed to be looking at pictures. Why are you so interested in getting to know me?"

"It just so happens, I checked your computer's history," Leah says. "The day before your accident, someone spent a hell of a lot of time researching Rebecca, blogs, reviews, her obituary. I seriously doubt it was Tim. He didn't know she existed before you woke up claiming to be her."

"So?" Alyssa says with a glance to her left. "What does that prove?"

Leah leans in and points at her. "You knew Rebecca was dead, not to mention every aspect of her life online a day before you were in the accident. Tim says you tried to call her brother Steven just before the crash." Leah takes a slip of paper out of her pocket and shows it to Alyssa. "Recognize the top number?"

Alyssa looks at it and seems to remember it. Then she looks to her left and back to Leah and says, "Not ringing a bell."

"You called that number several days ago," Leah says. "It rings to a Russian fellow. Sergei. Told me someone called him looking for Rebecca Asher. Why on Earth would you be trying to call a dead woman, two days before your accident?"

"I guess we'll never know," Alyssa says. She glances to her left, then points to a box with a green lid. "What's in that box?"

Leah sighs and picks up the box and reads what's written on top. "Photos from your senior year through the summer." She sets the box on the table in front of them.

Alyssa looks in the box. Right at the top is a shot of Alyssa and Rebecca standing with their arms around one another among a crowd of teens on a beach. They're holding cups and wearing bathing suits in front of a banner that reads "Fort Lauderdale, 1999!".

Alyssa holds up the photo. "You want a connection? Here you go. Connection established."

"What is it?" Leah asks, leaning toward her.

Alyssa hands Leah the photo. "There's me, and — I guess — me."

Leah takes the photo and examines it. "You're partying like it's 1999."

"Because it was!" Alyssa replies. "The year we graduated. As I recall, we puttered all over the place in my ancient Toyota."

"I remember you mentioning that you were driving down to Florida with your friends, Mandy and Sandy," Leah says. "Why aren't they in the picture?"

"I guess someone had to take it," Alyssa says.

"It doesn't take two people to take a picture," Leah says. "One of them should be here, at least. Sandy, probably, since you were so close."

Alyssa glances to her left, then sits back and crosses her arms. "I'm sure they were there somewhere. They were her friends, not mine." She looks to her left. "The Three Musketeers."

"Three Musketeers?" Leah says. "Interesting you'd bring that up, since, as you say, they weren't your friends."

"Maybe I'm just hungry. Do we have any candy bars?"

"You don't eat candy," Leah says.

"No candy?" Alyssa says, once again looking to her left. She turns back to Leah. "Where's the fun in that?"

"Your friend Sandy is living with her parents, I understand," Leah says, as much to herself as Alyssa. "I should arrange to drop in on her."

"She's still at home?" Alyssa says with mild interest.

"No, back at home," Leah says. "I heard she got married, but things didn't work out."

Alyssa glances to her left, then says, "Who's Doug?"

"Doug?" Leah says. "I didn't mention anyone by that name."

"Well that's a good thing, because I don't know who he is anyway," Alyssa says.

Alyssa is on the upstairs landing in her home in Lawrenceville, sitting on the floor, looking through the railings at the scene below. Leah's there, dressed in black, as is everyone else. It's the first time Alyssa has seen Leah in a dress since her older sister was in high school. Jolene, her uncle Duane's wife, and Viola, married to her uncle Boyd, are conversing just below Alyssa and she can only see the tops of their heads. Alyssa hears Jolene murmuring, "It's a good thing Paxton put a stop to that mess her family was trying to do." Viola starts to answer, but Jolene cuts her off, "This is enough of a pain without them adding their silly Jew rituals."

"Jolene!" Viola replies with a flustered voice. "Show some respect."

"Duane and I don't have time for this," Jolene says. "We need to be at my family's place in Mobile by eight."

Alyssa doesn't know Jolene or Viola very well, having only dealt with them on a family excursion to Hancock County over the previous summer, but her impression of them from the trip is that Viola is a sweet but somewhat scattered woman, while Jolene struck her as phony. Most of what she's learned about them comes from her aunt, Margaret, a reliable conduit for all the family's gossip. Like her father, Alyssa calls Margaret "Peg", whereas Leah calls her "Margaret", as did their mother. Viola is a dark-haired woman, about average in height, but thin and mousy in appearance. Margaret has described her as a "tragic Southern heroine," socially prominent, but whose father squandered most of the family fortune on booze, gambling, and women, before dying heavily in debt and leaving the family destitute.

Jolene is a full-figured woman with platinum blonde hair, who appears to be in her late-forties, originally from Mobile, Alabama, who bills herself as a style consultant. She met Duane at UGA and Margaret describes her as a "social climber who was looking to latch onto the most prominent man who'd give her a second look." Duane was "the perfect mark," analytical and bookish, without much experience with women before heading off to college. Alyssa's mother, Melinda, didn't have a very high opinion of Jolene either, calling her "racist and anti-Semitic" and unloaded on Jolene in private not long after they'd interacted. Paxton's decision in college to pursue being an architect instead of taking over their family's business, meant that it fell to Duane to assume the reigns from their father, but he never felt comfortable being in charge, so he convinced Boyd, more of a natural businessman, to run it jointly. Being the wife of a prominent business owner has inflated Jolene's opinion of herself, in Margaret's words, "to astronomical heights." Duane and Jolene do not have any children, and Leah has stated it's because Jolene doesn't want them. Of all the members of Alyssa's family, it's Leah who dislikes Jolene the most, and makes little secret of it, recalling at least once in Alyssa's presence that Jolene often antagonized Leah as a child for being too much of a tom-boy. Jolene has spread rumors throughout the family that Leah's a lesbian.

It has been not quite a week since Melinda died at their home, and her family, all observant Jews, are very upset with Paxton for not allowing them access to her body, waiting too long to get her in the ground, and for letting the medical examiner perform an autopsy to determine cause of death, which was a cerebral aneurysm that ruptured. None of Alyssa's aunts nor their husbands from her mother's side of the family are present, choosing instead to wait at the synagogue, where Paxton did arrange with Melinda's rabbi to conduct a traditional service. Leah found herself pulled into the conflict between Paxton and his inlaws, and Alyssa senses the toll it's taking on her older sister, who is suffering terribly because of their mother's death. Right now, Leah's standing near the large picture window, looking out, tears staining her cheeks.

Jolene and Viola stroll closer to the center of the room, allowing Alyssa to see them. Jolene fixes her eyes on Leah, shakes her head, then approaches Leah. "What is wrong with you? You need to be strong for your little sister, Leah. You ought to be upstairs right now consoling that poor girl."

Leah collects herself and turns to look at Jolene, and though she's clearly upset, she manages an angry smile. "How I choose to deal with my family is none of your business, Jolene."

"Why don't you act like a lady once in a while?" Jolene says. "I can't imagine your mama raised you to be like this."

"You leave my mother out of this," Leah says. "I never heard you say two kind words about her. Don't act like you even care."

"Somebody's got to look after that little girl," Jolene says. "I can't imagine that's going to be you, though, is it?"

Leah throws up her hands. "You know what? I don't give a flying fuck about you or your worthless opinions. Get out of my face, Jolene."

Jolene reacts with shock and moves away from Leah, who walks out of the room, still very upset. Alyssa hears the front door open; from outside the room, Paxton calls out Leah's name; the door closes. Paxton says, "Where's she going?"

From below, Alyssa hears Jolene say to Viola, "Did you hear what the dyke said to me?"

Viola gasps. "Hush, Jolene. That's totally uncalled for. She's lost her mother, too."

"I just want this over with," Jolene says.

Alyssa wishes she could comfort Leah, but she's been told by Paxton to stay in her room until Margaret picks her up. She wants to attend her mother's funeral, to say goodbye, but Paxton decided it would be too traumatic for her.

She still can't believe it's true.

She'd been sitting on the floor in the living room, watching *Clarissa Explains it All*, while her mother was cooking dinner. In the episode, Clarissa was trying to make a cake for her parents' anniversary, but things weren't turning out as she planned, much to Alyssa's amusement. Paxton was playing golf, as he usually did on Sunday afternoon and was due home within the hour. They were having spaghetti for dinner — Alyssa's favorite — and the smell of garlic and onions filled the house. Melinda came in, with her hand above her eyes. "Aly, could you keep an eye on dinner? I feel another migraine coming on and need to try to get ahead of it."

"Sure, Mama," Alyssa said, "I'll watch dinner for you. Feel better, okay?"

Alyssa rose and gave Melinda a kiss before heading into the kitchen. It was the last time she ever saw her mother.

Sometime later, Paxton arrived home. Finding Alyssa in the kitchen, he said, "There's my big girl, making dinner. Where's your Mom?"

"Mama's upstairs," Alyssa said. "She has a headache."

"I'll go check on her," Paxton said.

He was gone a very long time. Alyssa started to wonder about it, but before she could check, the doorbell rang. Alyssa found

Margaret outside, seeming unusually subdued. "Aunt Peg! Are you joining us for dinner?"

Before Margaret could answer, Paxton's voice came from behind Alyssa. "Your mother's not feeling any better, Princess. She may need to go to the hospital. Why don't you grab a change of clothes? Peg's going to take you to her place and get you to school tomorrow."

"Okay," Alyssa said.

Margaret followed as Paxton led Alyssa upstairs to her room in the middle of the hall. She gathered some clothes and her books. Back in the hall, she glanced at the master bedroom at the end. "I want to check on Mama before I go."

Paxton and Margaret exchanged a worried look, and Paxton said, "That's not a good idea just now. Your mother's resting."

"Oh," Alyssa said. "Well, tell her I love her and hope she feels better."

Paxton crouched beside Alyssa and gave her a tight hug, which Alyssa found odd. "I sure will, honey."

As strange as that scene had been, it did not compare to the surprise Alyssa had the next day, when she arrived home. Alyssa recalls every sound, word, and image, as she will for the rest of her life. She's walking up the walkway outside her home. The car pulling away from in front of her house and into the driveway across the street honks and she turns and waves to Sandy and her mother, who just dropped her off. She goes up the four steps to the porch with her key in her hand, unlocks the door. She starts to call out to her mother but hears someone moving around in the living room and heads there. Someone is there, but not who Alyssa expects. It's Leah, her back to the door, with her hand over her face. The family had been planning to go to Boston for Leah's graduation from Wellesley. Alyssa puts her hands together and bounces up and down.

"Leah, what are you doing here?" Alyssa says. "Why aren't you in Boston?"

Leah glances over her shoulder at Alyssa but does not turn. "Alyssa? You're early."

"Is Mama here?" Alyssa asks.

Leah seems to be wiping her eyes, then she turns to face Alyssa. "No, she's not here right now."

"Is she at the hospital?" Alyssa asks.

Leah moves toward Alyssa. "Did Dad bring you home?"

"Why would Daddy bring me home?" Alyssa asks.

"How'd you get here?" Leah says.

Alyssa shrugs. "There was something going on at the school

and they let us out early. I rode home with Sandy and her Mom like I usually do when Mama or Mrs. Joiner doesn't take us. The school sent a note home yesterday."

Leah stops and considers this. "A note?"

Alyssa looks around. "Is Mama still in the hospital? Are we going to go see her? Is that why you're here?"

Leah won't look at Alyssa. "Dad was supposed to pick you up. He needs to tell you something."

"Tell me what?" Alyssa says. She starts to worry. "Where's Mama?"

The phone rings. Leah answers, then her voice takes on a harsh edge. "Yeah, I know Dad, she's here. She said something about a note. Oh, now you remember. No, I haven't said anything. Okay, but please hurry. She's asking a lot of questions."

Leah puts down the phone and won't face Alyssa, who approaches her. "Leah, what's going on? Is Mama in the hospital?"

"No," Leah says quickly. "Dad's going to be home soon. He'll talk to you."

Alyssa becomes upset. "Why does Daddy need to talk to me? What's wrong with Mama? Why can't I see her?"

Leah puts her hand on Alyssa's shoulder and tries to guide her to the couch. "Come over here. Let's sit down."

"I don't want to sit down," Alyssa says, stomping her right foot. "Tell me what's going on. Where's Mama?"

Leah kisses Alyssa on the forehead and gives her a long hug. She releases Alyssa and takes her hands. "Mom's dead, Aly. It — it happened yesterday. Dad wanted to tell you himself. When we were together."

Alyssa is very upset. Leah attempts to comfort her, but Alyssa pulls away. "No! You're lying! I saw her yesterday. She wasn't feeling well but she's going to be okay. Stop lying to me!"

Alyssa runs out of the living room and up to her room. A short while later, Paxton arrives and confirms everything Leah said, which Alyssa already knows is true because why would Leah make it up? Later, Paxton tells her he wants her to go to Margaret's instead of the funeral. He and Leah argue over this decision, one evening in his study, with Alyssa listening outside, without their knowledge.

"You're a coward, that's what you are," Leah says to Paxton. "Afraid to face your responsibilities to me or Alyssa."

"Oh, I'm not a responsible parent, is that what you're saying?" Paxton replies. "I guess all the clothes and food and education wasn't enough for you, Leah."

"All you do is shovel money at everything," Leah says. "When were you ever there for me emotionally."

"I have a company to run and I'm a business leader in this city. That comes with lots of responsibilities."

"You knew Alyssa was leaving school early the day after Mom died, didn't you?" Leah says. "You knew when you insisted we all be together when you told her. But who was it who ended up telling her?"

"You were supposed to wait," he says.

"And you were supposed to be there," Leah screams. "But no. You were outside, sitting in your car. Mrs. Murphy said she saw you pull up out front just as she and Sandy were walking into their house, and you were still there ten minutes later. She was going to come over and see how you were, but then you pulled into the garage."

"I'm sure she's mistaken," he says. "I often sit in my car to collect myself before coming inside."

"Not parked on the street you don't," Leah says. "Even if that was true, she confirmed it was the same day she heard about Mom which is why she remembered it."

"What do you want, Leah?" Paxton says.

"I want my trust fund," she says. "I want you to sign it over, so I can be done with you."

"You'll get it when you turn twenty-five," he says. "Those are the provisions."

"Yeah, and there's a provision that states that the funds can be dispersed at any time after I'm twenty-one, if the custodians say so." Her voice cracks as she says, "You're the only custodian left."

"Fine," Paxton says. "You want the money, you can have it. Just don't expect anything more from me after that."

"I never have, and I never will," Leah says.

Alyssa wipes her eyes and allows the memory to fade. Ten or fifteen minutes after Leah's departure, she hears the front door open again and the reaction of those in the hallway signals Margaret's arrival. She also argued that Alyssa should go to Melinda's funeral, but Paxton was totally opposed and would not be moved. Margaret enters the living room dressed in black but wearing a colorful scarf and surveys the area. Alyssa has always noted how much Leah resembles their aunt in more ways than just looks. At times, when Margaret and Leah are out together, people mistake Leah for her daughter, and she's often very slow to correct them. Margaret exits into the hallway that leads to the kitchen, and returns several minutes later, as though looking for someone, concerned.

"Where's Leah?" she says to no one in particular.

Jolene glances at Viola, and says, loud enough for everyone in the room to hear, "Guess Butch went to be with her Jew family."

Margaret stares at Jolene with a look of outright fury, then goes to her and slaps her hard, causing her to crumple to the ground with a loud shriek. Viola is shocked, and Alyssa hears Duane and others react from outside in the hallway. Standing over the fallen woman, Margaret says, "If you ever call her that in my presence again, I will cut your tongue out."

Duane comes in, shadowed by Paxton and Boyd, and says, "What the hell, Peg?"

Margaret turns toward him, still furious. "Is there something you want to add to this, Duane?"

Duane surveys the scene, then looks away from his big sister. He throws up both hands. "No, ma'am."

He goes to look after his wife as Margaret moves toward the stairs. Paxton crosses his arms and stares at Margaret as she passes him but says nothing. Alyssa hops up and hurries into her room for her suitcase.

"Alyssa?" Margaret calls from the foot of the stairs. Alyssa emerges from her room. By the time she descends to where Margaret is waiting, Jolene is on her feet again, her makeup a mess, with her hand to her face; she's giving Margaret a murderous look, but she's silent. Once Alyssa joins Margaret, they depart without another word. They spend the afternoon talking about Melinda. When Alyssa returns home, Paxton informs her that Leah has returned to Boston. It will be many years before she sees her sister again.

Rebecca takes out a small stack of photos and starts sorting through them. Among them is a photo of Leah, around age eighteen, with a young Indian woman, and they're wearing caps and gowns. Alyssa, seated on the arm of the couch beside Rebecca, gets excited and points to the photo. "Ooo! It's Gitanjali Ramachandra!"

Rebecca holds up the photo. "Gitanjali Ramachandra."

Leah stares at her a moment. "What did you just say?"

"Gitanjali Ramachandra," Rebecca repeats. She glances at Alyssa, then finishes. "It popped into my head when I looked at this photo."

She hands it to Leah.

"This is Gita," Leah says, looking over the photo. A thought occurs to her. "Anything else pop into your head about her?"

Rebecca glances at Alyssa who considers it a moment, before saying, "She lived across the street in Buckhead. Her father worked for Bickering Plummet. She was Leah's best friend at Pace." Rebecca repeats this, then gives Leah a curious look.

"I shouldn't know that, should I?" Rebecca says.

"Rebecca shouldn't know it, that's for sure," Leah says. "You used to repeat Gita's name over and over when you were little. Drove everyone crazy. Except Gita. I think she encouraged you."

"Why did Alyssa do it?" Rebecca says.

"You just liked saying it." Leah places the photo on the table. "Let's try a little experiment, shall we? I'm going to ask you some questions and I want you to answer them quickly. Go with your first instinct."

Rebecca shrugs. "Okay."

"Why did you call Margaret Peg?" Leah asks.

Rebecca looks at Alyssa, who shrugs. "I don't know. I just did." Rebecca turns back toward Leah. "Who's Margaret?"

"Why were you going to Braselton?" Leah says.

Rebecca glances at Alyssa, who says, "Whatever Steven said, I guess."

Rebecca looks back to Leah. "Something to do with Kim Basinger."

"What about her?" Leah says.

"I don't know," Rebecca says. "Maybe I just wanted to see if she carved her initials in something."

"What's the first car you remember your parents owning?" Leah says.

Rebecca throws up her hands. "First car? What the hell?"

"Oh, come on," Leah says. "Every little kid remembers that first new car the folks brought home. For me it was a 1975 two-toned Cadillac Seville. Wire wheels. Power everything. Paxton Walker's reward to himself for his first six-figure development deal."

Alyssa remembers something and snaps her fingers and suddenly Rebecca is standing in the driveway of a large house, the lawn perfectly manicured and other large homes nearby. Rebecca thinks, *Buckhead*. Alyssa stands a few feet ahead of her, but now around four or five years old and holding the hand of a man whose face Rebecca can't see. They're looking at a new silver Mercedes as Alyssa bounces up and down and yells, "Take me for a ride, Daddy!"

Rebecca says, "A silver Mercedes?" The scene fades.

Leah smiles. "So, you are in there, Princess. Your memory seems oddly selective, though." Leah starts to ask another question but stops and examines Rebecca closely. "Why do you keep looking to your left?"

"What?" Rebecca says, restraining the urge to look at Alyssa. "I don't know what you're talking about."

"Yes, you do," Leah says. "Every time I ask you something, you look to your left. You see something, don't you?" Leah considers it. "Something. Or someone. Who is it?"

Rebecca glances at Alyssa, who says, "No secret's safe with the Sorceress."

Rebecca turns back toward Leah. "It's Alyssa. Not as I knew her. Much younger."

"How much younger?" Leah says with much interest.

"About. Ten?" Rebecca glances at Alyssa, who nods. "Yeah, ten."

"Age ten," Leah says out loud, but to herself.

"And that's important because?" Rebecca says.

"It's when our mother died," Leah says.

"Stevie was ten when our mother died," Rebecca says.

"Was he?" Leah says. "That has to mean something, then. Makes me wish I studied harder in Psych class at Wellesley." A thought comes to her. "Ask your Alyssa how a fugue state works. She's a teacher. She has to have had some psychological training."

Rebecca nods and turns to Alyssa. "So?"

Alyssa leans in closely to Rebecca. "There once was a beautiful princess who lived near a magical creek called John's. One day, far from home, she met an enchantress."

"She's telling me a story about a princess," Rebecca says.

"Can the fairy tales, Princess; they're not helping," Leah says.

Suddenly the Voice speaks with force. "Tell her it's not supposed to be easy and she knows it."

Rebecca looks all around. "Okay. Okay. Just calm down."

"What's she doing?" Leah says.

"It's not her, it's the other person," Rebecca says.

"You see another person?" Leah says.

"I don't see her; I hear her," Rebecca says. "It's like Aly's voice but really intense."

"Then what did she say?" Leah says.

"She said it's not supposed to be easy and you know it," Rebecca says.

"All right," Leah says. "Here's a question for whichever one wants to answer it. What's this all about? Why are you doing this?"

Alyssa leans in close and speaks to them both, and Rebecca

relays what she hears. "The Princess has fallen under a spell. To break it, she must accomplish three goals. Protect the boy; reconcile with the fair maiden; confront the dragon. Once these are done, she'll find her way home."

"A boy, a fair maiden, and a dragon," Leah says. "Can we be anymore cliché?"

"What do you think it means?" Rebecca says.

"The boy must be Steven Asher," Leah says. "You made a bee-line for him the moment you woke up. As for the others, the fair maiden is probably this Clarabella you keep going on about. The dragon, who knows? Could be a person. Could be something lurking in your past."

"It's all connected to me, right?" Rebecca says. "Rebecca, I mean."

"Which makes no sense whatsoever," Leah says. "Why would you need to fix someone else's life? Especially someone who's dead. Did you leave anything unfinished?"

"I was twenty-four," Rebecca says. "My entire life was unfinished."

"Connections need to be made," Alyssa says. "Relationships formed." Rebecca repeats this to Leah.

"What does that even mean?" Leah says.

"Literary crap," Alyssa says and Rebecca repeats.

"Literary," Leah repeats. "Figures. You've always liked your fairytales, Princess. Most standard fairytales are metaphors for some underlying psychological state."

"What do you mean?" Rebecca says.

"Like when you're worried about a test, and you have dreams of being naked, or something like that," Leah says. "For someone who loves them so much, it makes sense Alyssa would use them to try to communicate. Wish I'd studied them more."

Alyssa suddenly jumps up from the arm of the couch and rushes over to a stack of boxes. She points to a small box with a red top. "Tell her to look here. That will help."

Rebecca rises and goes to the stack. She removes the box with the red top and hands it to Leah. "She seems to want you to look in here." Leah opens it and removes a diary. "What is it?"

"Alyssa's diary from high school," Leah says. "This will be a big help. Thanks, Princess."

Rebecca goes back to the couch and drops onto it, falling back and letting out a sigh.

"What is it?" Leah says.

"It just hit me that in a few days, Alyssa's going to snap back into being herself and I'm going to cease to exist again," Rebecca says.

Leah takes her hand. "What happened to Rebecca was a tragedy. But you're not responsible for that. Whatever happens in a few days, Rebecca will still be dead. You have friends and family of your own, Princess, and they miss you."

"I guess it's good I don't remember how it happened before," Rebecca says. "I probably won't feel it this time either, but still, it's a little discouraging."

Alyssa runs over and sits on the arm of the couch again. "Nobody dies as long as someone remembers him or her. Mama said that. I'll always remember you."

Rebecca nods to her.

When Leah arrives back in Boston, Dan picks her up at Logan and she fills him in on the details of her trip home. She is still very upset about it a few days later, so Dan decides she needs something to shake things up and get her mind off her troubles.

"You need to stop being Leah for a while," Dan says.

"What are you talking about?" Leah replies.

"I'm heading to that big improv fest in San Francisco," he tells her. "Hitting all the little regional gatherings in between. Should take several months. I think you should come with me. Let's take Dander and Leander on the road."

"You're kidding, right?" Leah says. "I'm pretty sure we've already established that I'm not really an improviser."

Dan shakes his head. "What are you talking about? You're great."

"Dan, there's a vast difference in doing a few one-off scenes in front of a friendly audience and performing at a festival in front of seasoned improvisers," Leah says.

"See? That's just what I'm talking about," he says. "You're being Leah again."

"In case you haven't noticed, that's kind of who I am," she says. "What about MIT?"

"What about them?"

"I can't just blow off an accelerated Ph.D. program, as competitive as it is," she says.

"Who says you have to?" he says. "Write them a formal letter, explain your situation and request a hardship deferral."

"I can do that?" Leah asks.

"Sure, they understand that life happens," he says. Leah looks skeptical. "Hey, obviously they want you there. Didn't they recruit you?"

"They did," she says. "I don't know. Six months can be a long time."

"Do you really think you're ready to dive into the grind of an advanced degree right now?" he says.

She shakes her head. "About as much as I'm ready to spend six months on the road performing."

He stands and takes her hands, pulling her to her feet. "Come on! Let's hit the road. Have some fun."

"What about expenses? Hotels? Airfare?" she says.

"Forget all that," he says. "We're hitting the road in my Accord. It's big enough to sleep two."

"That old clunker?" she says. "You can't be serious."

"Think Bohemian for a change," he replies. "Step outside your comfort zone. Camp grounds, seedy motels, places Leah would never step foot inside."

Leah walks away from him, deep in thought.

"You know I'm right," he says.

Leah turns back. "Okay sure. Let's do it."

It takes about a week for her to defer her admission until January 1992, and to make arrangements with a garage for her car and to put some furniture and other items into storage. Finally, they pile into Dan's Accord and take off.

The tour, such as it is, takes a meandering route through the Midwest to places where improvisation has caught on; British reruns of the show *Whose Line is It Anyway* have been running on cable comedy channels, reigniting interest in the format. Early on, they meet with success in a few locations in Chicago and Milwaukee, but most of the "clubs" they find themselves in are church basements with a hodgepodge of performers, with more of a variety format than pure improv. Here, Leah and Dan ditch their regular act of Leah being a patron Dan pulls out of the audience, to both of them appearing on stage together as a team. Leah is actually relieved; while she doesn't consider herself a strong improviser, the informal settings allow her to relax, since compared to some of the local acts on the bill, she seems like a polished professional. When they finally make it to San Francisco for the week-long festival, she returns to her role as the "volunteer" Dan calls on to assist him at each show. While she earns some praise as the straight man to Dan's zany characters, several of the other performers are surprised when they learn she's a regular part of the act.

Throughout the tour, Leah is in the habit of calling home to talk to Alyssa every few days. She's not happy at the way she left things between them following their mother's death, and hopes that by staying in touch, she can somehow convey how much she still cares for her sister. Late in the year, while she and Dan are in Los Angeles, Leah dials her family's number one afternoon, and Paxton answers.

"Hi, Dad. Is Alyssa there?" Leah says.

"No, she's spending the night with her friend Sandy," Paxton says.

"Sorry I missed her," Leah says. "Tell her I said hi. Talk to you later."

"Leah, wait," Paxton says. "I took a call for you this afternoon from MIT."

"MIT called there?" Leah says.

"They say they've been unable to reach you directly," he says.

"Yeah, I've been sort of incommunicado," Leah says. "What did they want?"

"Your deferral ends next month and they need to know what your plans are," he says.

"Has it been six months already?" she says. "I'd like to know what my plans are."

"So, you're just going to give up on all your educational goals?" Paxton says.

"Why do you care about my goals?" Leah says.

"Leah, I know we've always had our differences, and I realize, I haven't been much of a father to you," he says.

"That's the understatement of the year," Leah says.

"I deserve that, I suppose," he tells her. "But you've always seemed so self-sufficient, I just felt — well, never mind how I felt."

Leah sighs. "Is there a point to all this?"

"You were always so much closer to your mother and I'm sorry she's not here to talk to you about this," he says. "I'm a poor substitute, I know, but despite our differences, there's one thing I've always admired about you, Leah."

Leah is caught off guard. "What's that?"

"In everything you do, you may fail, but you never give up," Paxton says. "Now, if traveling around the country, doing this performance thing is what you truly want to do with your life, I'll respect that and wish you the best of luck. But something tells me you want something more for yourself. I think if your mother was here, she'd tell you the same thing."

Leah does not immediately respond.

"Leah?"

"Yeah, I'm here," she says. "Do you have the information from MIT?"

"Yes. I heard from Ms. Crocker in the Registrar's office," Paxton says. "I don't have the number in front of me."

"I'll figure it out," she says. "Ms. Crocker. Got it."

"Take care, Leah," Paxton says.

"Dad?"

"Yes, Leah?"

"Thanks a lot," she says. "I really do appreciate it."

"Not a problem, Leah."

She concludes the call just as Dan enters. "Leah, I have got some great news."

"What is it?" she says.

He sits near her, leans forward, and points both index fingers at her. "Remember that guy at the improv jam on Thursday, Jay?"

"The bald guy who didn't recognize me from our set?" she says.

"Yeah, him. Turns out, he's from Second City in Chicago," Dan says.

"You're kidding."

He moves to beside her and put his arm around her shoulder. "And that's not all. He sat in on our show last night and he's very interested."

"In us?" Leah says.

Dan nods. "Uh huh."

"As in you *and* me?" she says.

Dan doesn't look at her. "Sure."

"Right."

"Oh, okay, he's really only interested in me, but I told him we're a team," Dan says.

"And what did he say to that?" Leah asks.

"He wasn't quite as enthusiastic," Dan replies.

Leah nods. "Thought so. Look, Dan, improv is your dream, not mine."

He puts his hands on her shoulders. "You are much better at it than you think."

"Well, that's debatable but I can make this easy for both of us," she says. "Remember MIT? The deferral? Turns out they've been trying to get in touch with me."

"You're going back?" he says. "That's great."

"Looks like we both get to pursue our dreams," she says.

They hug.

"I'm really going to miss you," he says.

"Oh, I'm sure you're going to miss seeing me first thing in the morning with bed head after sleeping in a recliner," Leah says.

"Maybe not that so much," he says. "Come on. Let's grab a bite before the show."

Leah has been back in Atlanta for less than forty-eight hours when she receives the news that her aunt Margaret has died. Leah lost touch with most of her family after she left Atlanta following her mother's funeral in 1991, though she has tried to stay in contact with her sister. Feeling guilty over not calling more often, Leah phoned Margaret several months after starting at MIT, to apologize, only to be told by Margaret, "Don't worry about us, sweetie. You do what you need to do to become the person you're meant to be. We'll be here when you're ready."

That was in 1992. Leah defended her thesis late in 1997 and received her Ph.D. early in 1998, and at that time, checked in with Margaret, who was coughing a lot and thought she might have an upper respiratory infection. Leah made plans to return home and was looking forward to reconnecting with family. Recalling Margaret's words from when she started at MIT, Leah feels certain her aunt understood her silence, but Leah still regrets not being here.

In an angry call to her father the afternoon before, Leah took him to task for failing to keep her informed.

"Thanks a lot, Dad, for letting me know about Margaret," she said.

"I tried calling the number I have on you in Cambridge, but it was disconnected," Paxton said.

"Oh. Yeah," she said. "I moved out last month."

"Peg was only diagnosed two months ago and started treatment right away," he said. "The prognosis wasn't good. The doctors said her condition was terminal from the beginning, but the treatment was supposed to buy her a little time."

"What happened?"

"She contracted pneumonia," he said. "The treatment weakened her immune system. She didn't last long afterward."

"I should have been here," she said.

"You're here now," he said. "Do you have the address of the church?"

"Yeah, what's up with that anyway?" Leah said. "When was the last time either of you were in a church?"

"It's what she wanted," he said. "I didn't understand it, but I respected her wishes."

"Is Alyssa around?"

"She's at a birthday party for her friend Mandy," he said.

"I guess I'll just see her tomorrow, then."

The following morning, Leah puts on her dark business suit with slacks, and heads to the church. Upon entering and giving her eyes a moment to adjust, the first person she sees is Alyssa, much taller than Leah remembers her, milling about in the vestibule. When Leah enters, Alyssa looks at the door, and once the light returns to normal after the door closes, allowing her to see who's come in, Alyssa approaches her sister. "Leah?"

"Hey Princess," Leah says. She gives Alyssa a quick hug. "It's been a long time. Wow, you're getting tall."

"Dad said you called," Alyssa says. "I wasn't sure if you'd heard about Aunt Peg. It all happened so fast. One day she was a little under the weather, a week later, she had terminal cancer."

"That's what Dad said," Leah says. "Precisely why I stopped smoking. Dad should take a hint." She touches Alyssa's shoulder. "How've you been?"

"I'm okay," Alyssa says. "Are you still in school?"

"No, I graduated," Leah says. She leans in. "I'm a doctor now. I just got back to Atlanta."

"Are you working anywhere?"

"Not yet, but I have some ideas," Leah says. "I may go back to school. You're going to be a senior, right?"

"I will be. Yes."

Leah moves a few steps toward the sanctuary. "I suppose Dad looks about the way I remember him. Sounded the same."

"A little older," Alyssa says. "He grew a beard."

"You don't say," Leah says, facing her.

"Were you really traveling around doing improv?" Alyssa asks.

"At first, yes," Leah says. "Not after I went to MIT."

"I find it very difficult to imagine you doing something like that," Alyssa says.

"I'm a woman of many talents," Leah says with a chuckle.

An usher looks out from the sanctuary. "Miss Walker?"

Alyssa looks at him, nods, and tells Leah, "I guess they're ready to start."

"Okay if I sit with you?" Leah says.

"I'm sitting with Daddy," Alyssa replies

"I figured. We can tolerate one another a little while for Margaret's sake," Leah says. They head into the sanctuary together.

A few days after the funeral, Leah drops in on an old acquaintance at the downtown offices of Walker Development, LLC, the firm founded by her father around the time she was born. Walt Blankenship is the only board member still left that Leah remembers. She phoned the day before to get the name of the receptionist, hoping to get into the office without having her presence announced.

The day she visits, she phones from outside to be sure the same receptionist is on duty, then follows a deliveryman in and uses an old hacker trick of walking into the office with her briefcase, as though she's supposed to be there, while the receptionist is occupied, holding her phone so that it partially obscures her face.

"Morning, Cheryl," she says as she passes the desk.

"Oh. Ah. Morning," Cheryl says, glancing quickly in Leah's direction while dealing with the delivery. Once she's in, Leah heads for Walt's office on the second floor.

"How's it going, Walt?" she says leaning in from the doorway.

Walt looks up then rises. "Leah! How did you get in here without someone buzzing you up?"

"You know me," she says. "Nobody can keep me out of someplace I really want to be."

He waves her in, then meets her halfway and embraces her. "How long has it been?"

"Too long, Walt," Leah says. "How're the years treating you?"

"Can't complain," Walter says. "I'll be getting out of here middle of next year and I have a whole bevy of grandkids I need to start spoiling."

"I bet you're looking forward to that."

They head to the sofa near the window and sit.

"I haven't seen you since before you left for college," Walt says. "I hear you're Dr. Walker now."

"Not among friends," she replies. "I'm still Leah."

"So, to what do I owe this pleasure?" he asks.

"I hear you're looking for a senior network engineer," Leah says.

"We are," he replies. "That sound like something you could handle?"

"Definitely."

"Then the job's yours," he says.

Leah shakes her head. "No, Walt. I don't want to get this job based on who I am. I want it because of what I know." She takes a copy of her résumé from her briefcase and hands it to him. "I want you to submit this to the search committee."

Walt takes it and looks over it. "L. J. Rosales? Rosales was your mother's name, wasn't it?"

"Yes, it was," Leah says. "Since my credentials are under my name, you can verify them without involving the others on the committee, and work out any issues with HR."

"You understand, Leah, you'll be under the same level of scrutiny as any other applicant," Walter says. "If you can do the job, why does it matter how you got it?"

"It matters to me, Walt," Leah says. "As a woman, I already face enough of an uphill battle without people dismissing me because I'm the founder's daughter."

"We'll do it your way, then," he says.

"I don't want you to pull any punches with me either, Walt," Leah says.

"Not to worry," he says. "The upstarts on the search committee don't take my input seriously anyway. They'll hire you just to spite me." They rise, and Walt extends his hand. "Good luck, Dr. Rosales."

Leah learns she's one of the finalists for the position. Several days later, she finds herself in a board room with the search committee seated at a table before her. The interview goes well, and the committee is impressed with her knowledge and responses, with the exception of Walt who nitpicks her lack of real world experience. Despite this, when the chair polls the others, most vote to hire Leah, with only Walt voting against.

Once she's in charge of the network, Leah initiates a total overhaul of the system, catching several serious errors including an accounting glitch where building supplies were being recorded at their discount cost rather than full price, which made it seem the company was spending less than it actually was, and a software error that would have caused the system to crash if the database exceeded a certain size. Before long, she makes herself indispensable to coworkers and company officials. Settled in, she enrolls in the Ph.D. program at Georgia Tech, and purchases a home in the "transitional" neighborhood of Kirkwood. She's at her terminal one afternoon when someone enters her office and says, "L. J. There's someone I'd like you to meet."

Leah rises and turns to find herself face to face with her father, with one of the office managers.

"Paxton Walker, L. J. Rosales," the manager says.

"L. J. Rosales?" Paxton says, giving her a curious expression.

Leah extends her hand. "Mr. Walker. It's an honor to finally meet you."

Paxton chuckles and shakes her hand. "Good to meet you, L. J. Nice to put a face with a name."

"Mr. Walker," the manager says, "you should know, Dr. Rosales has been nothing short of a miracle worker. To say she's saved us from millions in potential losses is an understatement."

"Impressive," Paxton says. "Keep up the good work — Doctor."

Paxton and the manager turn to leave. As he's exiting, Paxton looks over his shoulder at Leah, then shakes his head, with a smile. Leah collapses into her chair and breathes a sigh of relief.

Several months later, at the annual company picnic, Leah is outside talking to a coworker when Alyssa appears, escorted by an employee. Seeing Leah, Alyssa says, "Why's my sister here?"

"Who's your sister?" the employee asks.

"The woman in the emerald green top," Alyssa says.

"That's L. J. Rosales, our network engineer," the employee tells her.

"Rosales?" Alyssa says. "That was our mother's name." Suddenly, Alyssa realizes what's going on. "Oh, wait. Never mind. My mistake."

"L. J. Rosales is your sister? Paxton Walker's daughter?" The employee steps away from her. "Excuse me." The employee exits, quickly.

Leah sees Alyssa and walks over to meet her. "Alyssa."

Alyssa shakes her head. "Sorry, Leah. I think I blew your cover."

Several employees appear with the one who'd been with Alyssa. They point and whisper among themselves.

"Perfect," Leah says, amused. "Thanks a lot Princess."

Leah heads up the walkway of the Murphys' house in Lawrenceville, here to see her sister's best friend from high school. Leah didn't know most of Alyssa's friends, but the Murphy family lived across the street, so Leah would see them whenever she was home from college. Her last real interaction with them was at her mother's funeral in 1991, and since then, she's only heard them mentioned by Alyssa on occasion. After Alyssa went away to college, Paxton sold the family home in Lawrenceville, and purchased a condo in Atlanta, near the golf club where he played at least twice a week, and, several weeks earlier, suffered his fatal heart attack.

Reading Alyssa's diary, Leah has learned that while she was in Florida with her friends Casandra Murphy and Amanda Joiner, Alyssa met Rebecca Asher. Wanting to better understand Alyssa's relationship with Rebecca and getting very little tangible information from Alyssa other than the weird fairytale instructions, Leah hopes to learn from Sandy what happened on the trip, to cause what Alyssa describes as "the worst situation ever between me and Sandy," one that might "end our friendship."

Alyssa didn't elaborate beyond that, though she does recount several things they did there. Alyssa's diary is the first time Leah is aware of any tension between Alyssa and her friend. She hopes to learn from Sandy what part Rebecca played in it.

She's met at the door by a dark-skinned black woman dressed in yoga pants and an Emory University sweatshirt. Her hair is long and curly, and pulled back by a bright orange headband.

"Leah Walker," she says.

"Casandra Crowley," Leah says.

"Just until my divorce is final," Sandy says, as they shake hands. "I'm taking back my name. I've thought about changing the kids' names, too."

"That bad, eh?" Leah says.

"We'll see," Sandy replies.

The living room Sandy leads Leah into is strewn with toys and children's clothing. Space has been cleared for them on the couch and resembles an oasis amid the sea of clutter. They sit, and Sandy takes Leah's hand. "I am so sorry to hear about your father. Mr. Walker is one of those towering figures from my childhood."

"Dad was larger than life, that's for sure," Leah says.

"On top of that, for Alyssa to be in a car accident," Sandy says. "I can't imagine what your family's going through right now."

"It's been a rough month," Leah says.

"I apologize for the mess," Sandy says, motioning around the room. "Mom and Dad took in me and the kids after Doug headed to California, and since he asked for the divorce, they're letting us stay here rent free until I finish my degree and get a job. I try to tidy up while the kids are at school, but sometimes that's easier said than done."

"No problem," Leah says. "Did Alyssa know your husband?"

"Yeah, Doug and I dated in high school, then applied to the same college when we graduated," Sandy says.

"Your mom gave me an overview of that part on the phone," Leah says. "I had heard you'd gotten married, but I didn't recall the details."

"I was one of those girls who thought it would be cool to marry my boyfriend before we went away to college together," Sandy says. "When our daughter, Andrea, came along not quite two years later, we agreed it would be best for Doug to get his degree first, then I could go back when Andi was older. After our son Cliff was born, Doug graduated, found a job on the west coast and decided that maybe we shouldn't have gotten married so young. He informed me of this just as we were preparing to join him."

"I hope he's at least supporting you and the kids," Leah says.

"So far he's been good about that," Sandy says. "He got a really nice job once he graduated. It's where he met his current girlfriend which I think had more than a little to do with his decision." Sandy pauses, then says, "I've seen photos of him with her on Facebook. Seems he found someone more his complexion."

"Say no more," Leah says.

"On the phone, you said you wanted to talk about our trip to Florida," Sandy says. "I haven't thought about that in years."

Leah has decided not to get into the details about Alyssa's condition. Instead, she says, "Alyssa's having some memory issues because of the accident. The doctors thought it would be good if her husband and I could help reconstruct as much of her past as possible. I found her diary, so I thought I'd start there."

"I see," Sandy says. "She always had such a great memory. I'm happy to tell you what I can recall, but to be honest I don't have very fond memories of that trip."

"I'm sorry to hear that," Leah says. "What happened?"

Sandy leans forward. "It was supposed to be our big adventure together, me, Aly, and our friend Mandy. We'd sort of been the three musketeers since Mandy showed up in third grade and this was going to be our first grown-up outing."

"In her diary, Alyssa says she met someone on the trip to Florida," Leah says.

"Yes. Rebecca," Sandy says, less than enthused.

"You remember her?"

"I can't forget her," Sandy says. "At the time, I thought the girl was coo-coo for Cocoa Puffs."

"Really."

"Aly and I had a major falling out over Rebecca," Sandy says. "I'm sorry to say, I was on the wrong side of it."

As Alyssa suspected, Mandy and Sandy's reaction to having Rebecca join them is mixed. When she and Rebecca find them on the beach, Mandy is her usual, affable self, welcoming Rebecca and quizzing her about where she's from and which school she attends. Sandy seems uncharacteristically aloof, hardly speaking to Rebecca, but shooting questions at Alyssa privately about what she knows about this newcomer. From the start, Sandy is convinced she's seen Rebecca before, but can't pinpoint where.

As they attend various activities around town, Sandy continues to be suspicious of Rebecca's motives and recommendations.

Rebecca is interested in trying out some of the smaller events, where there are fewer people but more local acts, while Sandy wants to go places they can be seen and hear known bands. Alyssa also has to help Rebecca out occasionally, slipping her cash whenever it's her turn to pay, since Sandy has suddenly become concerned about each person taking an equal part in footing the bill for their activities. On one occasion, they argue over who'll be appearing at a venue.

"I heard *NSYNC is going to be there," Sandy says.

"No, they're not," Rebecca replies. "They're in Cancun for MTV's Spring Break. That's where all the major acts are."

"Well I heard differently," Sandy says. "Some folks on the beach know the promoter."

"There would have been an announcement," Rebecca says. "They're a huge act. If they were here, the promoters would want people to know."

"It's supposed to be a surprise show," Sandy says.

"Yeah, the surprise is, *NSYNC isn't performing," Rebecca says. "Show runners always spread rumors to get people into their venues, because they can't be held legally responsible for unsubstantiated rumors."

"How do you know all this?" Mandy asks.

"I know people who book shows in Atlanta," Rebecca says. "The concierge at your hotel told me it's some lounge band from Miami headlining the show tonight."

"It still sounds better than sitting in a stupid coffee shop listening to somebody we're never likely to hear from again," Sandy says.

"The Indigo Girls used to play small venues in Atlanta," Rebecca says. "Now they're headliners."

"Look, we can check out the beach first, and if nothing's happening, we can go someplace else," Mandy says.

"Exactly," Alyssa adds. "No need to get into an argument about it. You two need to relax and try to get along."

To Alyssa's dismay, the tension between Sandy and Rebecca continues to grow, and she and Mandy constantly have to intercede to diffuse situations that threaten to escalate to more than uneasiness. When Rebecca isn't around, Sandy complains about how she's interfering with the trio having fun, and about Alyssa being too quick to pay tabs for Rebecca.

"It's my money, Sandy," Alyssa tells her. "It's not that much or very often. She covers stuff when she can."

"It just seems very convenient that she would show up out of the blue like that," Sandy says. "And now she has you paying for her? You don't find that a bit suspicious?"

"We've talked about it," Alyssa says.

"You've talked about it," Sandy says. "Fine. I guess that makes it all okay, then."

It all comes to a head toward the middle of the week when Sandy tells Alyssa and Mandy she has something important to tell them when Rebecca arrives. Once she's there, Sandy wastes no time in confronting her.

"So, Rebecca," Sandy says, "tell us again how you found Aly's purse at the restaurant. Where exactly was it?"

Alyssa confronts Sandy. "Why are you bringing this up again?"

"There's a lot you don't know about her, Aly," Sandy says. "She's a liar and a thief."

"Hey!" Rebecca says.

Sandy turns to Rebecca. "Go ahead. Deny it. I remember now where it was I saw you. It was at the seafood place when Aly lost her purse."

"What?" Rebecca says.

"What are you talking about?" Alyssa asks, looking between Sandy and Rebecca.

Sandy crosses her arms. "While we were there this girl sitting in the booth behind you and Mandy got up and left. I didn't see her face, but she had dark curly hair and was wearing a Braves jersey, with Chipper's number." She points at Rebecca's jersey. "Like that one. Remember, I yelled out 'Chipper!'"

"Yeah, I wondered why you did that," Alyssa says.

"She had that bag over her arm, just like now," Sandy says. "It looked like she was trying to hide something."

"Andy," Alyssa says just under her breath.

"I told you how I found her purse," Rebecca says.

"Yeah, and you're lying," Sandy says.

Alyssa moves between Rebecca and Sandy. "That's enough, Sandy."

"Why are you even wasting time with her? We're your friends. Not her. You're so much better than she is," Sandy says. "She's not worth the trouble."

"Sandy!" Alyssa says.

"She's a loser, Aly," Sandy yells, "a white trash loser. Why can't you see that?"

Mandy gasps. "Whoa."

Rebecca lowers her head. "Excuse me." She leaves.

"I can't believe you just said that — and in front of her," Alyssa says. "What's gotten in to you, Sandy? Maybe she rubs you the wrong way, but what you did was cruel."

Alyssa heads to the door.

"Aly, where are you going?" Sandy says.

"To find my friend," Alyssa says. She exits into the hallway and takes the elevator down to the lobby, where she finds Rebecca sitting on a couch near the entrance. Alyssa sits beside her.

"I am so sorry for what she said," Alyssa says. "For what it's worth, I don't think that way about you."

"It means a lot to me," Rebecca says. "Aly, you know I would never do anything to hurt you, right?"

Alyssa doesn't immediately respond but seems to be mulling over something. She finally says, "Becky, I know Sandy's telling the truth about how you acquired my purse. Or at least, her version is closer to the truth than yours."

"What do you mean?" Rebecca says.

"The day we met, when we were at the coffee house, you slipped once and called me Andy," she says. "You probably didn't think I caught it, but I did. At the time, I convinced myself I must have misheard you, but when Sandy said she saw you at the restaurant, I knew I hadn't. They only call me Andy when it's just the three of us, so there's only one place you could have heard them."

"If you knew, why didn't you call me on it in the room?" Rebecca says.

"I don't know why you took my purse, or what your plan was in returning it, but you returned it," Alyssa says. "Since then, you've been a pretty decent friend."

"It doesn't bother you that I never pay for anything?" Rebecca says.

"Trust me, my father is not hurting for money," Alyssa says. "It's a small price to pay for the pleasure of your company."

"I wish I got along better with your friends," Rebecca says. "Well, friend, I guess."

Alyssa shakes her head. "I have never known Sandy to be like this. It's a side of her I don't like very much."

"She just doesn't like sharing you," Rebecca says. She puts her arm around Alyssa. "I can understand that."

Until the end of the week, Alyssa and Rebecca spend time away from Sandy and Mandy, and when Rebecca leaves the day before Alyssa, they exchange numbers, agreeing to stay in touch. For their last evening in Florida and the following day, during the ride back, Alyssa and Sandy hardly speak, instead relaying messages through Mandy. A month later, when they graduate, they're still not speaking.

"**Aly** was very disappointed with me," Sandy says. "Mandy stuck with me, but I could see she was disappointed, too. I was pretty mad at them both, but in the time in between, I've come to be disappointed in myself. I've learned that no amount of artificial privilege my parents' economic status bought for me can change how people perceive me and I know how it feels to have doors slammed in my face. I didn't like Rebecca. She lied. She was manipulative. She made everything about her, all the time — but she was a human being. I should never have regarded her as trash and Aly was perfectly right to take me to task for that. If only I had realized it sooner. I might never have lost my best friend." She dabs her eyes with the sleeves of her shirt. "I've always wondered what happened to Rebecca. Do you know?"

"She was a writer who worked for Creative Loafing and maintained her own blog," Leah says. "From what little I've read of her stuff, she was really good."

"Was?" Sandy says.

Leah nods. "She died in a senseless car crash not quite five years ago."

Sandy lowers her head. "God rest her soul."

Leah sits forward and rests her chin on her fist. "As far as you know, did Alyssa have any contact with Rebecca after she got back home?"

"If she did, she didn't share it with me," Sandy says. "We didn't confide in one another at all after that trip, but I don't recall Rebecca's name coming up from Aly or Mandy."

Leah takes Sandy's hand and squeezes it. "Thank you so much, Sandy. This really helps."

"Next time you see Alyssa, tell her I'm thinking about her," Sandy says. "I really miss her."

Leah takes out a card and writes on the back of it. "Now's not the best time, but once Alyssa's feeling a little better, you should arrange to go by for a visit. I know she'd love to see you again." She hands Sandy the card. "Here's her number. Her husband Tim can keep you updated. Call and introduce yourself."

"I'll do that," Sandy says.

That's *one potential fair maiden*, Leah thinks as she walks back to her car. *Protect the boy.* She takes out her phone and dials a number. A man answers. "Steven Asher, this is Leah Walker. I understand you've met my sister, Alyssa."

"That's correct," Steven says. "A version of her at least."

"If you're free tomorrow, I'd love to talk about it," she says.

"Sounds like a date," he says. "If you don't mind, I'd like to invite my aunt, Rachel, and Becky's friend, Claire."

"The more the merrier," Leah says. "How about noon?"

Oakhurst

The house at 466 East Lake Drive, is a two-story pre-War unit with a full porch. The exterior could use a coat of paint, but otherwise, it's well-maintained and in excellent shape. When Owen Asher signed the closing papers on it in late summer of 1985, it was a dingy gray color, paint peeling and flaking, and several of the posts on the steps and railing around the porch were broken or missing, the windows were boarded up, and the lawn was overgrown. The house had stood empty since the original owner died with no heirs around 1980, and the county auctioned it to cover the property taxes. The entire area was depressed, still suffering from the effects of "white flight" in the 70s, when many white families relocated from the interior of Atlanta to the Northern and Western suburbs of Gwinnett and Cobb counties in response to school integration and the changing complexion of their neighbors.

Starting in the mid-80s, a number of enterprising individuals, among them, Owen Asher, saw the potential in the area and took advantage of the low prices to secure a home. Owen bought the house from the third realty company that owned it for around $65 thousand, citing the condition of the property and neighborhood to talk them down from the asking price of $80K. Proximity to MARTA was a major selling point for Owen, who needed easy access to the airport, having taken a job with Air Atlanta, his first job flying with a commercial airline after being a cargo pilot. Following nearly two months of renovations, Owen, Sharon and Rebecca took possession in October, and Owen carried first Sharon, then Rebecca, who Owen called "Little Bit," over the threshold to celebrate.

Every morning, when Owen had a flight, Sharon would drive him to the MARTA station and send him off with a kiss before heading back to get Rebecca ready for school and get to her job as a teller at C&S Bank. One morning in 1990, a little more than three years after Owen and Sharon welcomed their son, Steven, Owen awoke well before Sharon and carried his bags out to a waiting cab which took him directly to the airport. Sharon's surprise at finding Owen gone that morning was greatly amplified few hours later, when a process server showed up at the bank to present Sharon with divorce papers. It was her first notice that something wasn't right in their marriage. She spent the afternoon sobbing to her sister Rachel on the phone while nine-year-old Rebecca looked after Steven in his room, wondering what she'd done to drive her father away. The house went to Sharon in the divorce settlement, with one provision being that the remaining mortgage was paid in full by Owen in lieu of spousal support, Sharon only requesting support for the kids, and upon her death, it went into a trust for Rebecca and Steven, managed by Rachel. When he turned twenty-one in 2008, as the only surviving heir of Sharon Elizabeth Asher, Steven inherited the property.

Leah pulls into the driveway at 466 East Lake Drive in her Porsche 911 and parks beside the blue Honda Civic already there. Surveying the residence as she walks around to the front door, she estimates its value at well over $300K. The location isn't far from a home she once owned and sold in Kirkwood a few miles west. Steven greets her at the door, wearing casual slacks, an Oxford shirt with the sleeves rolled up, and loafers.

"I appreciate you taking the time to see me, Steven," she tells him, once she's inside. "I imagine this is all pretty weird for you."

"Weird?" he replies. "Anywhere from six to twelve times an hour I get a call from this woman whose voice sounds nothing like my sister's, but with all Becky's attitude and quirks of speech. I had to turn the phone off because it was too distracting."

"I'm hoping, if we put our heads together, we can figure out why the Princess is acting like this," Leah says.

"Princess?"

"It's what I call Alyssa," Leah says.

"Then you don't think this is about Becky," Steven says.

"Rebecca figures into it, somehow," Leah says. "I'm stumped as to why Alyssa has taken on her personality and shows such an interest in your family. Obviously, they knew one another, but I haven't found evidence that they interacted very much."

"I'll tell you what I can about Becky," he says, "but before Alyssa left that message for me, I'd never even heard her name."

"What's the status on your aunt and Rebecca's friend?" Leah says.

"Rachel and Claire will be here shortly. Claire just called and said they're leaving Rachel's now."

"Perfect," Leah says as wanders around surveying the living room and surroundings. "I read a little of Rebecca's blog the past day or so. I find I rarely agree with her opinions, but I like her prose style — very direct and in-your-face."

"That's Becky," Steven says, sitting against the arm of the

couch. "A publisher was interested in doing something with her blog, but she died before she'd compiled very much. I've thought about shopping her work around to a small publisher, or self-publishing — if I ever have time to work on it, that is."

"Let's hope you do," Leah says. "Her feminist critique of the work of Bette Davis was a little lacking in details, but she definitely brought a fresh perspective."

"Yeah, she really liked Bette Davis," Steven says.

She looks around at the house. "This is a nice place. I can see you've done some work recently."

"I'm trying to convince my girlfriend to move in," he says.

"Full basement?" she asks, to which he nods.

"Partially finished with a separate entrance," he replies. "I'd like to rent it out if I can get it in shape and find something to do with the pool table that's down there now."

"A young, upwardly mobile family would pay a fortune for a place like this," Leah says.

"I'm sure they would," Steven says. "I plan to have an upwardly mobile family myself one day. What would you like to know from me?"

Leah stops pacing near the couch and sits. "Everything I know about Rebecca comes from what I've read by or about her. I need to know the real Rebecca to sort out what she represents to Alyssa. How does her version compare to what you know about Rebecca?"

"She knows enough to convince me she spent quite a bit of time with Becky," Steven says. "If I had to guess, though, she probably spent more time with her when Becky was younger. She changed a lot after she went away to college."

"In what way?" Leah says.

"Take her voice, for instance," Steven says. "When she was away at college, Becky perfected sounding like Bette Davis. She always loved how Davis talked, so she practiced. When she watched an old film, she'd repeat back lines in Davis' style of speech. At Columbia, Becky finally nailed the speech patterns, so it sounded natural and not forced. Alyssa sounds like she's imitating Becky."

Leah nods. "Do you know of the feminist author, Andrea Dworkin? Rebecca's photo sort of reminds me of her."

"I've heard the name," Steven says.

"But you don't know what she looks like," Leah says.

He shakes his head. "Nope. Sorry."

"So, let's talk sisters," she says, sliding to the edge of the couch and turning so she's facing him. "On the day before her accident,

Alyssa spent an extraordinary amount of time reading up on Rebecca. She appears to have read everything Rebecca wrote, and just about everything written about her, warts and all."

Steven slips from the arm down onto the couch, at the opposite end from Leah. "You found all this on her computer?"

"I'm an Internet security consultant," she says. "It's my understanding that you were ten when your mother died. Is that correct?"

"It is," Steven says.

"Alyssa was ten when our mother died," she says.

"Interesting coincidence," Steven says.

Leah leans forward and focuses ahead of her, like she's picturing something. "Let's break this down. Assume Alyssa learned about Rebecca's death a day or so before her accident. She spends hours reading up on Rebecca, then tries to contact you just minutes before she's in a car accident herself. And the first thing she does when she wakes up—"

"Is contact me," Steven picks up the thought, "just like Becky would have."

"So, what was life like with Rebecca in charge?" Leah asks.

"More like I was in charge," he says. "Becky used to say she was in a rebuilding phase at the time. If Alyssa spent any time with my sister, she'd have seen how obsessive Becky was about staying in touch," Steven says. "Half the time she was calling me. The other half, it was Claire." He lowers his head. "On the day she died, when Becky suddenly went silent, I was sure something bad had happened."

"Tim said you identified her body," Leah says.

He nods. "Rachel offered to take care of all that, but I insisted. I just wanted to see, to know for sure."

Leah pats his shoulder. "It's tough being the responsible one." She takes out a slip of paper and hands it to him. "That reminds me. Do you recognize the top number? I know the bottom one is yours."

"Becky's cell phone," he says.

Leah nods. "Alyssa called the cell number a day or so before her accident, and when I looked it up, I found both numbers in my contacts log from 2005."

"Why would Becky have called you?" Steven wonders.

Leah shakes her head. "No idea. I was on my first big project for NSA back then. All my files are archived, but I rang up the cell number and reached a guy from Moscow named Sergei."

"Sergei?"

"Nice guy," Leah says. "Sells shoes at Lenox. Promised me a

sweet deal on some suede boots next time I'm in the area. When he found out I speak Russian, he talked my ear off. Tried to set me up with his brother-in-law. "

Steven finds this amusing. "What prompted you to learn Russian? Just curious."

"When I was a teen during the Cold War, this girl wrote to the Soviet premier to ask why he wanted to blow us up," Leah says. "He invited her over for a visit. I thought if I could speak it, I could get a free trip to Leningrad."

Steven seems skeptical. "Okay."

"Back to the point. Sergei said he used to get calls all the time for Rebecca Asher but only one in the past few weeks," Leah says.

"Alyssa," Steven says. "She must have tried to call before she did the research on the Internet. Becky's information is pretty easy to find."

"Yes, it is, and the things Alyssa looked up online contained a lot of background about Rebecca," Leah says. "Stories, reviews, her blog."

"The sort of information she wouldn't need if she knew Becky well," Steven says.

"Exactly," Leah says, pointing at Steven. "I have Alyssa's diary from high school and other than the time they spent in Florida, I can't find any evidence they interacted at all back then."

"In whatever way Alyssa came by the information, she definitely knows a lot about Becky," Steven says.

Leah rises. "Yes. Tim told me about your initial meeting." She goes to the credenza and picks up the photo of Rebecca. "From the way the Alyssa talks about her, it sounds like Rebecca's relationship with Claire was rather stormy."

"That's one thing I'm not clear on," Steven says. "Alyssa seems to believe that Claire and Becky were dating."

"They weren't?"

"Not at all," Steven says. "Knowing the types of women my sister typically associated with, I was surprised she and Claire were even as close friends as they were."

Leah puts down the photo of Rebecca and leans against the credenza. "To hear Alyssa describe her, Claire was the love of Rebecca's life."

"Maybe Becky thought so," Steven says. "Claire doesn't even identify as a lesbian. She's always claimed to be celibate. They did spend a lot of time together — and Becky had her pet name for her, 'Clarabella', which was unusual — but by the time she died, they were majorly on the outs with one another."

"Do you know why?"

"It could have been any number of things," Steven says. "Claire hated most of Becky's friends. They were always making fun of her when she wasn't around. I think they were intimidated by her."

Leah turns back to the photos and picks up the one of Owen. "This must be Owen the pilot." She looks at Steven. "I see the resemblance. Are you in contact with him now?"

"Yeah, he showed up at Becky's funeral," Steven says. "One of the few times I saw my aunt almost lose it. Since then, we've managed to rebuild our relationship."

Leah stares at the photo. "Who does he fly for?"

"He was with Northwest and went to Delta when they merged," Steven says.

Leah nods. "I've tried but couldn't get much out of Alyssa about your Dad. She tends to focus on the loss — a countenance more in sorrow than in anger."

"Becky was much angrier than sad," Steven says.

Leah puts the photo back and turns to Steven. "She doesn't recognize your father. She doesn't talk about your aunt. It's like she's very selectively recreating aspects of Rebecca's life while ignoring others. Very confusing."

Their conversation is interrupted by the sound of someone on the porch followed by a key in the lock. Leah says, "Rachel and Claire, I presume?" Steven nods.

Rebecca sits at the laptop in her living room. The computer is angled to catch much in the vicinity of the couch. In the background, Alyssa is dancing on the couch with her back to the camera and her head down with her hair covering her face. Music from rotation at WRAS, Georgia State's radio station plays in the background. Rebecca is heavily intoxicated. She'd gone shopping at Lenox to find a present for her brother Steven, and ran into Alyssa Walker, a friend she met in Florida in 1999. They've been at her house all afternoon watching movies, until they got through their second bottle of wine, and started listening to music instead.

"Here with my best bud. My soulmate. My— my—" She leans back toward Alyssa, "What are you anyway?"

With a scream, Alyssa jumps backwards off the couch and runs around so she's briefly out of the camera's range, then jumps in beside Rebecca and leans into the camera. She's also very intoxicated.

"Your long-lost sister!" Alyssa yells. She pulls Rebecca out of her chair, saying, "I like this song!" They start to dance. "What will your little brother say if he comes in?"

"Stevie's at our aunt's all week," Rebecca says.

"It's just that as much as you talk about Steven, I was hoping I'd get to meet him," Alyssa says.

"Maybe," Rebecca says with a bit of a giggle. "Someday."

"No doubt when we run into each other five years from now," Alyssa says.

"Yeah," Rebecca says. She likes the idea. "Let's do that. Five years from now, whatever we're doing, we'll drop everything and look each other up."

"That sounds awesome," Alyssa says. They dance around for a few moments.

"You know, Aly," Rebecca says in a seductive tone. "Usually when I bring a hot chick home and get her drunk, I plan to seduce her."

"You're not going to seduce me?" Alyssa asks.

With a slight laugh, Rebecca pulls Alyssa to her and gives her a long, passionate kiss. Alyssa complies without betraying how it's affecting her. Rebecca releases Alyssa who seems a bit stunned.

"That do anything for you?" Rebecca says.

Alyssa shakes her head. "No. Not really."

Rebecca shrugs. "I tried."

"What about this Claire you mentioned on the way over," Alyssa says. "I thought she was the love of your life."

Rebecca nods. "Wish I could convince her of that — my Clarabella! I'd show you a photo, but I don't have any."

"You don't have any photos of the love of your life?" Alyssa asks.

"Claire's very high maintenance," Rebecca says. "Hell, we both are — but she's always there for me, like no one I know. She's really touchy about having her picture taken for reasons I'm not at liberty to discuss. I could show you what she looked like in eighth grade, but she doesn't look anything like that anymore."

"I imagine not," Alyssa says.

Rebecca sighs and collapses onto the couch. "Well, hell, if we're not going to fuck, what else can we do? Dance. Watch another movie."

Alyssa has a thought and doubles over, laughing. "Hey, how about a prank phone call?"

"A little juvenile," Rebecca says. "But sure, we could do that. Who do you want to call?"

Alyssa snaps her fingers. "How about my sister?"

Rebecca gets the portable phone. "What do you want me to say?"

"Just something stupid," Alyssa says. "Oh, call her Lee. She hates it when people mispronounce her name."

Rebecca nods. Alyssa dials a number and hands the phone to her. She holds the phone so that Alyssa can listen in.

At the very moment Alyssa is dialing her number from Rebecca's home in Oakhurst, Leah is at her home several miles away in Kirkwood, communicating via speakerphone with her colleague, Roscoe Delahunt, who's helping her work out logistics on a project for the National Security Agency. Leah competed for the contract, with advice from Scoey, the previous year, and, upon winning it, brought him onboard as a subcontractor to help assemble and manage the team she'd need to carry out the work she's been assigned, protecting the phone system from a terrorist attack. Scoey brought together a group of the most notorious phone phreaks and hackers he could find, most looking to curry favor with the government, to combat federal charges pending against them. In the few months since starting the contract, Leah has acquired a detailed knowledge of the many ways a phone can be used for mischief by a malicious individual and collected a number of tools and tricks to break into a system and use it for nefarious purposes. Because she's also dealing with proprietary phone system data, she's had to sign a number of non-disclosure agreements, plus an agreement to hand over whatever tools are developed to the NSA, as well as any records uncovered.

Roscoe's melodious baritone, well suited for phone support, comes from the speaker on her cell phone. "So, anyway, Annabelle has been confined to a wheelchair since the early nineties."

"This place would be perfect for her," Leah says. "The folks who sold it to me had a son with cerebral palsy, so there's a ramp out front, and the doors are extra wide. I mean it's a nice place and a happening neighborhood, but I just hate the commute downtown every day."

"Tell me about it," he says. "That's why I work from home. No commute."

Leah's private land line rings. A caller ID box pops up on her computer screen. "Who the hell is Rebecca Asher?"

"I know her," Scoey says. "She's a local reporter and blogger. We haven't spoken for a while."

"Why's she calling the private line?" Leah says. "Think it's about the project?"

"Doubtful," he replies. "She does concerts, art openings, theatre."

"Mute your phone and open a chat window," she says. "Let's see what she wants."

"Sure thing," he says. A chat window pops up on her screen. He types, "What say we try out some of this fancy new cop equipment Uncle Sam loaned us?" Several programs open on her computer. She types back, "My thoughts exactly." Leah types in Rebecca's name and her address shows up on Leah's console. She clicks to answer the call and is greeted by a woman's voice that puts Leah in mind of Bette Davis. "Hey, Lee."

"Who's this?" Leah says.

"This is Bianca," the woman says.

Roscoe types, "It's definitely Becky's voice. She sounds like she's been drinking. Big surprise."

As Leah speaks, property and DMV records, police reports and other info on Rebecca appear on her computer. Scoey types, "I can probably get you her college transcripts if you so desire". Leah types, "Do it."

"Bianca?" Leah says. "That's not ringing any bells. How do I know you?"

"I met you in a club in East Atlanta," Rebecca says.

"Are you talking about Aunt Ivy's?" Leah says as she clicks icons and more info appears on her computer. "Say, wasn't the deejay Javier? Do you know if he's still the one spinning records at the club?"

"I don't know if Javier is still at the club," Rebecca says.

"Good to hear he has a fallback if the baseball doesn't work out," Scoey types.

"No, wait," Leah says. "I bet it was Class Action. The bartender's a skinny fellow with pink hair."

Scoey types, "I know that guy. He does my taxes."

"I don't remember anyone with pink hair," Rebecca says, confused. "That's not important."

"Okay, then, let's cut to the chase," Leah says. "Why are you calling?"

"You told me to call you sometime, so I'm calling," Rebecca says.

"Right," Leah says, starting to figure out what's going on. "You must be one of Alyssa's little friends. Put the Princess on the phone."

Roscoe types, "Princess?"

"Put who on the phone?" Rebecca says.

"Alyssa," Leah says.

"I don't know anyone by that name," Rebecca says.

As Leah speaks, Rebecca's credit card and school records show up on her screen. She types, "Good job, Scoey. I'll take it from here." To Rebecca, she says, "Who did you say you were again?"

"I told you, I'm Bianca," Rebecca insists.

"No, you're not," Leah says. "I know you're lying."

"Well aren't you a Miss Know-it-all?" Rebecca says, her voice taking on an edge.

"I know how to deal with drunk idiots like you," Leah says.

"What's that?" Rebecca says.

"Listen up, little girl," Leah tells her. "You need to sober up and stop playing out of your league, because trust me, you have no idea who you're dealing with."

Scoey types, "It's on now".

"I don't know who I'm dealing with?" Rebecca says, flustered. "Oh yeah. Well you don't know who you're messing with — bitch!" The line disconnects.

"Yep, that's Becky," Roscoe's voice comes from Leah's cell.

"What's her level of computer savvy?" Leah says.

"Slim to none," Scoey says. "She always relied on me for research."

"Know how we've been wanting to test out that dialer you swiped from the Russians?" Leah says.

"I like the way you think," he says. "Coming up."

A dialer opens on her console. She types in Rebecca's home number. "This should get your attention, Rebecca Jean. You got her cell number, Scoey?"

"Entering it now," he says.

Once it's entered, Leah sings, "Please allow me to introduce myself." She clicks "Go" and an icon that reads "Dialing" appears on the screen.

Rebecca slams down the phone, and she and Alyssa start laughing. "Your sister sounds like a real bitch."

"She's very sure of herself," Alyssa says.

Suddenly, Rebecca's cell phone starts ringing. Rebecca looks at it. "What the fuck?"

"What is it?" Alyssa asks.

"It says it's coming from my home number," Rebecca says. "From me." Alyssa shrugs. Rebecca presses the speaker button. "H-Hello?"

Leah's voice comes over the phone. "Hello again Bianca. Or, should I say, Rebecca Jean Asher at 466 East Lake Drive, Decatur. Just curious, how did you enjoy your time at Columbia University?"

"Columbia?" Rebecca says, then looks at Alyssa. "How do you—"

"Not much, apparently, since you didn't finish," Leah says. "You're still going to have to pay off those loans you know. Uncle Sam really hates it when you default, and it looks like you're hanging by a thread as it is."

"Who the hell is she?" Rebecca says to Alyssa, who shakes her head.

"By the way, your cable bill is overdue," Leah says, "but you probably don't want to use your Visa for that. It's just been reported stolen. Now take me off speaker and hand the phone to Alyssa."

Frightened, Rebecca does as she's told. Alyssa reluctantly takes the phone. "Hi, Leah. Yeah, I guess it wasn't very smart to use your private number, was it? Of course, I've heard of the Patriot Act. Really? Wait. You work for the Bush administration? I thought you hated— Oh, NSA. No. No, I wasn't aware you could do that. Less than a minute. That's actually really scary, Leah. Okay. I'll tell her. Bye now." She hangs up and says to Rebecca, "She says if you call her again, she's going to have your electricity shut off and reroute all the radio station request lines in North Georgia to your cell phone."

"She can do that?" Rebecca says.

Alyssa nods. "Yeah, she's like a sorceress."

Rebecca sighs, then says, "Okay, you probably should have mentioned your sister's a fucking phone phreak *before* we made a prank call to her."

The front door opens, and two women enter. The first appears to be in her late-forties or early-fifties, with feathered, dark hair that's streaked with silver that hits her shoulders. She projects a calm demeanor, thoughtful and introspective, and bears a slight smile. Above average in height, she appears to be in good shape, with conditioning that reminds Leah of people who do yoga. She's wearing jeans, running shoes, and a tank top with a carryall over one shoulder. Following her, is a woman who appears to be in her thirties, who's much taller, with long, straight, dark hair that's pulled back into a ponytail. She's wearing a black T-shirt that reads "WRAS 88.5" with jeans, red and black checkerboard Vans and a dark baseball cap with no logo, and a chain wallet. She's also in very good shape, lean and toned, reminding Leah of some of the women in her martial arts class. The older woman greets Steven with a hug and a kiss on the cheek and the younger woman gives him a one-armed hug.

Steven introduces the older woman as his aunt, Rachel, and the younger one as CC Belmonte. As she's shaking hands with Leah, CC says, "Claire".

"Clarabella," Leah says, which surprises Claire.

"That was Becky's nickname for me," Claire says.

"I've heard quite a bit about you," Leah says. "Which leads me to suspect my sister, Alyssa, also heard quite a bit."

"Does she have a good memory?" Rachel asks.

"Near photographic," Leah says.

"Like I said, what she knew was scary," Steven says.

Claire points at him. "Before I forget, have you given any thought to next Friday?"

He nods. "Yes. I'm free and can attend your graduation show."

"Graduation show?" Leah says. "Acting? Singing?"

"I'm talking an improv class at The Comedy Factory in Midtown," Claire explains. "I run the boards for them, so they give me employee comps all the time."

"Dan Barton performs there, doesn't he?" Leah says

"He's my instructor," Claire says.

"He's an excellent teacher," Leah says. "Haven't checked in with him for a while. I need to look him up."

"Steven gave me an overview of the situation with your sister," Rachel says. "I find it very intriguing, from a psychological standpoint. I'm going to have lots of questions for you."

"Steven mentioned you're a nurse," Leah says. "Are you also a psychologist?"

"Yes, I have my doctorate in psychology, with a concentration in counseling," Rachel says.

"A nurse who's a doctor — impressive," Leah says. "You sound like just the person I need to talk to."

Steven polls everyone for drink requests and disappears into the kitchen. Claire and Rachel gather some chairs which they bring over to the couch. Once she's seated, Rachel says, "Understand, that without interviewing her directly, anything I say will be speculative. But whatever you can tell me would be helpful."

"I honestly don't know what to make of it," Leah says. "Alyssa's always been rather sensible, if, at times, overly emotional. She's a lot like our mother, actually. I forget that sometimes."

"What does she do?" Rachel says.

"She's a school teacher, first and second grades," Leah says. "In addition to thinking she's Rebecca, there seems to be some kind of weird fairy tale going on in her head."

"Fairy tale?" Rachel says.

Leah leans forward. "Claire, Steven tells me you and Rebecca were not dating. Is that correct?"

"That's not how I would describe our relationship, though we did go out a lot," Claire says.

"Alyssa seems to think you were the love of Rebecca's life," Leah says.

"From Becky's perspective, maybe. Not mine," Claire says.

"Without getting too personal, you never gave Rebecca a reason to think so, correct?" Leah says.

"Not intentionally, that's for sure. How she chose to interpret my words and actions was up to her."

"You mentioned a fairy tale," Rachel says. "Tell me more about that."

"I can only tell you the things Alyssa has relayed to me," Leah says. "She claims she's Rebecca and knows a lot about her. She says she's accompanied by a younger version of herself, from around age ten, which is when our mother died. She also says there's a voice that makes pronouncements, Alyssa's voice, but cold and unemotional."

"And the fairy tales?" Rachel says.

"When I tried to have her version of Rebecca quiz the younger Alyssa on what a fugue state is, she started telling a story about an enchanted princess," Leah says. "She said to break the spell, she has to protect the boy, reconcile with the fair maiden, and confront the dragon."

"There's always a dragon," Claire says.

"That doesn't match with any psychological condition I'm familiar with," Rachel says. "Certainly not a classic fugue state and true dissociative personality disorder is extremely rare. It almost sounds supernatural."

"Alyssa has always been a fan of fairytales and make believe, but with a strong grounding in reality," Leah says. "I've reasoned that the boy is Steven, and the maiden may be Claire."

"Reasonable assumptions," Rachel says.

Steven enters with a tray containing a pitcher with water and four glasses. He sets it on the coffee table and returns to his seat on the couch. Rachel pours everyone a glass of water.

"Her association with Rebecca seems to have started when Alyssa went to Florida," Leah says, reaching into her pocket. She takes out the photo of Alyssa and Rebecca in Florida and hands it to Steven. "Ever see this?"

Steven takes the photo, looks it over, and nods. "I remember the trip." He hands the photo to Rachel who shows Claire.

"What can you tell me about it?" Leah says. Steven defers the question to Rachel.

"There's really not much to tell," Rachel says, sitting back and sipping her water. "I told her she couldn't go, and she packed up her car and went. Becky and I rarely saw eye to eye, even before she went to college. After she got back to Atlanta things got worse."

"For some reason, I have it in my head that Rebecca didn't graduate, but I can't say why I think that," Leah says.

"Becky dropped out her junior year," Steven says. "She never said why — to me at least."

"Defying what she perceived as my authority was a favorite pastime of hers," Rachel says.

"Perceived?" Leah says. "What do you mean by that?"

"Without going into too many details, my niece and I had more in common than she was willing to acknowledge," Rachel says. "We both wanted to strike out on our own, take the world by storm. How we did that may have been different, but the desire to get out there and experience life was common to us both."

"How did it manifest itself for you?" Leah asks. "If you don't mind my asking."

"Not at all," Rachel says. "Los Angeles, late seventies, adult entertainment industry. I think you can connect the dots."

"Rather wild time," Leah says.

Rachel laughs. "I was a rather wild person back then. So was my partner. I lost her in 1990."

"Drugs?" Leah says.

"AIDS," Rachel replies. She lifts her bag into her lap and removes a brochure. "While we're on the topic, I'm part of an organization called Journey From Night. We work with exploited women."

"I've heard of them," Leah says. "You do good work."

"We try. We're always looking for positive role models for the women we counsel. Perhaps you'd be interested in talking to them sometime."

"It'd be an honor," Leah says.

"We can sort out the details later," Rachel continues. "I tried to convey some of the lessons I learned to Rebecca, but she'd already made up her mind that I was the enemy." She drops her bag beside her chair. "I understand you've lost your father recently."

"That's right," Leah says. "Dad died second of August."

"Losing a loved one can be very traumatic," Rachel says. "How are you dealing with it?"

"In my own way," Leah says.

Rachel nods. "Sorry if I've overstepped."

"Trust me, I'll let you know if you overstep," Leah says. "Now, I said Alyssa's association with Rebecca started in Florida, but that's not entirely accurate. According to Alyssa's diary, she and Rebecca were both born at Northside Hospital on April 20, 1981."

"Really?" Steven says.

"That's very interesting," Rachel says. "And might give us some insight into what's caused Alyssa to become so invested with Becky."

"I thought so, too," Leah says. "Both Steven and Alyssa were ten when they lost their mothers."

"She could have learned all about that from Becky in Florida," Steven says.

"When she came back from New York, Rebecca was very troubled," Rachel says. "She wouldn't talk about what happened and wasn't an easy person to deal with by any means."

"I get this very disjointed picture of her," Leah says. "I've read her writing and she comes across as intelligent, if a bit full of herself. But, she was in her early-twenties, so I sort of expect that."

"Rebecca needed her mother," Rachel says. "I didn't fill the bill for her, unfortunately. She needed someone to lash out at and I was there. Growing up, Rebecca saw me as this mysterious aunt who lived on the West Coast. She was an imaginative child, probably built up lots of mystique about me. The reality never quite matches the fantasy."

"How did you feel when she was appointed Steven's guardian?" Leah says. "That couldn't have been easy for you."

Rachel shakes her head. "On the contrary. I stepped aside."

"Why?" Leah says.

Rachel leans back and links her hands in front of her. She looks away from Leah. "Rebecca learned about my past, which I wasn't really trying to hide, but which might have caused some friction. I'm not ashamed of what I did when I was younger. I lived it and I accept responsibility for the choices I made."

"Healthy attitude," Leah says.

"I'm honest with those around me about who I was and who I am," Rachel says. "Rebecca was determined to air that in court, and I was afraid it would damage her relationship with Steven.

So, I agreed to relinquish control, on the condition that she didn't cut me off from him."

"Did being his guardian help her?" Leah says.

Rachel nods. "At the time she died, Rebecca was starting to show signs she was turning things around. Maybe being Steven's guardian stabilized her a bit." She looks toward Claire. "Her friendship with Claire helped as well."

"Steven says his father showed up at Rebecca's funeral," Leah says.

Rachel nods. "Despite my best efforts. I wasn't happy, but he did seem genuinely contrite."

Leah takes out her cell phone. "So, Claire, I hear you don't like having your picture taken."

"I avoid it if I can," she says.

"Care to make an exception?" Leah says, holding up her phone. "I'd like to show Alyssa what you look like."

Claire considers it, then shrugs. "Fine by me, but I don't want to see it on Facebook."

"I'm not on Facebook," Leah says. She snaps a couple photos of Claire and Rachel. "If you're planning on being onstage, you'd better get used to having your picture taken. Speaking of which, has Dan ever talked about his days in Boston?"

Claire considers this. "Yeah, as a matter of fact, he has."

"I knew him then. We were a team for a few months on the road," Leah says. "It was just after I got out of Wellesley in the early 90s."

Claire puts her index finger up to her lips then shakes her finger at Leah. "Were you Leander? As in Dander and Leander?"

"Yes!" Leah says. "Those are the names we performed under. My forte was group think. Dan was better at characters."

Claire laughs. "He speaks very fondly of you, actually."

"He should," Leah says. "We were practically joined at the hip before we gave the act a merciful end in Los Angeles."

"I want to meet your sister," Rachel says.

"That can be arranged," Leah says. She turns to Claire. "But the person she really wants to see is you."

"I don't know about that," Claire says. "Becky and I weren't on speaking terms when she died for reasons I'd rather not dredge up right now."

"I won't press," Leah says.

"I guess it depends on which version of Rebecca she thinks she is," Claire says.

"Alyssa's version of Becky seems more like she was before she went to New York," Steven says. "She has facts from later, but her personality was more pre-NYC."

"I didn't know her then," Claire says. "She said we met once, but I don't remember. She followed a musical group I've worked with since the 90s, so if she followed them pre-NYC, it's possible our paths crossed." Claire considers the request for several moments. "I don't see the harm in meeting with her. It won't be what she expects, though."

"Perfect," Leah says. "I'll set something up."

"I'd like to observe, if we can arrange that," Rachel says.

"Works for me," Leah says. "Where and when?"

Steven is seated in the living room when the phone rings. He answers and is greeted by Rebecca's voice. "Hey, Goonie, where's the pizza that was in the fridge?"

"You mean the pizza that was in the refrigerator for three weeks?" Steven replies. "I threw it out."

Rebecca comes out of the kitchen, still talking on the phone as though Steven isn't there. "Why'd you throw it out? I was going to eat that."

"Becky, there—" Steven starts to answer on the phone, then stops himself, hangs up and speaks to Rebecca directly. "Becky, there was stuff growing on it."

"So? Just zap it in the god-damned microwave. That kills just about anything." She continues to hold the phone to her ear, though she's facing Steven.

"I can't believe you ever lived on your own" he says. "Did your roommates in New York take care of you?"

"What am I supposed to have for dinner now?" she says.

"Why don't you use one of the numbers on the refrigerator?" he says indicating the kitchen. "There are at least five pizza places."

"My credit card's not working again," she says.

"What's wrong with your card?" Steven asks.

"I don't know. It just keeps getting declined," she says.

"You paid them, right?" he says. "You're supposed to do that every month, you know."

"Oops!" she says, covering her mouth.

He sighs. "Order whatever you want. I'll pay for it."

Rebecca gives him thumbs up. "Yes! Yea, Stevie!"

Leah has just asked about the pool table downstairs, so the discussion moves to the basement, which is a large, open, almost loft-like space, with a small kitchenette, a full bath, a large pantry, and separate bedroom. There's a utility closet for the water heater and furnace. Rachel brings down some snacks, and Leah asks if Steven has anything more potent to drink. He retrieves a bottle of wine and a glass for Leah, beers for himself and Claire, and a soft drink for Rachel. Leah tries out some practice shots, before Claire challenges her to a game. As they play, Rachel quizzes Leah about her family and sister.

"Privileged is an understatement in our case," Leah says. "As a child, I wanted for nothing, except the one thing that wouldn't have cost my father a penny."

"His affection," Rachel surmises, to which, Leah nods. "You were a child of the seventies, weren't you? Father worked, Mom tended house."

Leah acknowledges this. "Mom spent her entire married life as a housewife to an influential real estate developer. If she had lived, I have no doubt that, after her children were raised, she'd have finished her degree and pursued something she cared about. She knew the value of being a positive influence."

"When did you lose her?" Rachel says.

"I was twenty-two," Leah says. "I was about to graduate college."

"I sense your father wasn't much comfort," Rachel says.

"You could say that," Leah says. "He's largely the reason my sister and I haven't been as close since then. He had a large influence on her."

"Seems to be a theme," Claire says. "You do not want to hear the history of my family, mother or father."

"One thing I can say about my father is that he was pretty transparent," Leah says. "Not much lurking in his closet. He worked too much to have any time for personal scandals."

"Would you say you inherited his single-minded determination?" Rachel says.

"In my industry, I need every bit of determination," Leah says. "I learned early on it's better to stand one's ground and be thought a bitch than to roll over and agree with something you don't like. Ironically, with me in charge of Dad's estate, I now have a voice on the board of his company, so I'm damn well going to use it when need be, even though I've always had a love/hate relationship with the business."

"Sounds like there's a story there," Steven says.

"The company was born on the same day I was," Leah says. "It got all Dad's attention, until Alyssa came along."

"How was your relationship with your sister growing up?" Rachel says.

"As close as two siblings can be, who are separated by twelve years," Leah says. "When she was little, I think she regarded me as one of the adults."

"Would you say you're more your father's daughter?" Rachel asks.

"I probably have more in common with Dad," Leah says, "though neither of us would have admitted it, especially to one another."

In between turns on the pool table, Leah surveys the basement, making suggestions for improvements if Steven's planning to rent it out.

"Structurally," she explains, "the space looks sound, but it doesn't feel very livable."

She walks over and taps a square column in the center of the living room. "Ah. Hollow. This isn't load bearing, I'm guessing. Maybe it's concealing pipes."

"Get rid of that and you'd open up the whole space," Claire says.

"Exactly," Leah says. "With all the windows, a nice, bright paint job might also eliminate the need for so many lights down here." She points to the walls. "Get rid of the paneling, put in some track lighting. It wouldn't necessarily break the bank and the improvements would pay for themselves with your first tenant."

"I'll give it some thought," Steven says.

"You're pretty handy, judging by the other work you've done upstairs," she says. "I'd recommend professionals for the wiring and structural changes, though. I know a number of people who'll give you a fair price and do good work." She leans on the pool table. "Do any of you know why Rebecca left school?"

"I suspect Owen was involved," Rachel says.

"Owen the pilot," Leah says, mostly to herself.

"Yes, that's what Sharon called him," Rachel says. "Rebecca picked it up from her. He'd been making overtures for several years after he learned Sharon had died. I kept him away from them as best I could — intercepted letters, turned away phone calls."

Indicating Steven, Leah says, "I assume that changed after Rebecca's funeral."

Rachel nods. "I decided I wouldn't try to interfere with any relationship Steven wanted to have with him, though I can hardly bear to be in the same room with Owen."

"I think that's my cue to check something upstairs," Steven says, then exits.

Leah watches him leave, then says, "Not willing to forgive?"

"I tolerated him for Steven's sake," Rachel says, "but I can't forget what he did to my sister and niece. He had the audacity to look me up when he moved to the West Coast. Thought he'd take a crack at the older sister."

"Really?" Leah says. "What'd you do?"

Rachel chuckles. "Let me put it this way, when I later told him he couldn't have access to Steven or Rebecca while I was in the house, he didn't press it."

"Good for you," Leah says.

"I had no control once Rebecca was out of the house, however," Rachel says. "She never indicated any desire to resume her relationship with him, but that wouldn't have stopped him from trying."

"I take it she never confided in either of you what happened," Leah says.

"She told me she failed out of her final semester, but didn't go into details about why," Claire says.

Rachel nods. "She was in New York, blazing a trail through Columbia, then, suddenly, she dropped out, showed up at the house, and dived right into the bottom of a bottle."

"What made you suspect her father had something to do with it?" Leah says.

"Aside from Sharon, he was the only one who ever had any power over her. As much as she complained about him, I think she never got over wanting to know why he left them — left her."

"In that, I can sympathize," Leah says. "Although, I was in the unique position of having an absentee father who was always present."

From above, Steven calls down, "Is it safe?"

"Yes," Rachel says. "We're back to the rant-free zone."

"Anyone need anything?" he says.

Rachel looks at Claire, then Leah, who says, "Water?"

"Bring some water," Rachel calls up. Steven acknowledges this.

"I have to say, I am very impressed with that young man," Leah says. "With all the tragedy he's endured, he seems remarkably together."

"Steven has a good head on his shoulders," Claire says. "I liked hanging out with him whenever I'd visit Becky."

"I wish he'd take more time to enjoy himself," Rachel says.

Steven descends with a pitcher and glasses on a tray. Rachel relieves him of the tray and circulates around to everyone.

"I'm a little angry with myself for not being better acquainted with Rebecca's work, before now," Leah says. "I wasn't reading Creative Loafing in the early-oos."

"Her writing was the one area that never suffered, even when she was having problems," Claire says.

"She was pretty scathing in her criticism of that last festival she attended," Leah says.

"Want to hear something funny?" Steven says. "The Festival renamed their closing ceremonies and awards presentation in her memory."

"Really?" Leah says.

"They called here to complain about her review," he says. "When I told them about the accident, they felt guilty and asked if they could honor her. I figured it's the kind of thing she'd get a kick out of, so I said yes. Over the years, they've totally upgraded everything and it's really prestigious now."

"Oh yeah," Claire says. "We've been several times. We always get the VIP treatment."

"Since I feel like the conversation is veering away from the main topic, can we agree I'll bring Alyssa over on Thursday to meet with you, Claire?" Leah says.

"That's acceptable," she says. Rachel indicates she's available, too.

"I'm scheduled to take the bar exam that day," Steven says, "but since Claire and Rachel have keys, they can let themselves in. Say, do you have any influence with Walker Development?"

"A bit," Leah says. "What's up?"

"They've been sniffing around here, asking about this place," he says. "I've fended off several offers from them and other real-tors. I've told them no, but they're very persistent."

"I'll see what I can do," Leah says with a wink. She takes out her phone and dials. "Hey, Cheryl, L. J. Walker here. Who's in charge of acquisitions these days? Bradshaw. Put me through to him, if he's available." She clicks to put her phone on speaker.

"Tom Bradshaw," the man answers.

"Hello, Tom, L. J. Walker here," Leah says.

"Yes, Ms. Walker, what can I do for you?" he says.

"Dr. Walker," Leah says, which amuses Claire and Rachel.

"My apologies, Doctor," Tom says. "How can I help you?"

"Did I meet you at my father's funeral?" Leah says. "There were so many people there, I lost track of them all."

"Ah, no, I wasn't able to make it," Tom says. "I believe the department sent flowers, though."

"I'm sure they were lovely," she says. "I understand we're looking at a piece of property on East Lake Drive. House number 4-6-6."

"Let me take a look," he says. The sound of fingers on a keyboard can be heard. "Oh, yes. Research says the owner's dead and one of her kids is living there."

Steven shakes his head and points to himself.

"Yes," Leah says. "That house is off the market."

"Are you sure?" Bradshaw says. "Do you have any idea what that place is worth?"

"As a matter of fact, I do," Leah says. "The owner isn't dead. His name is Steven Asher and he was born and raised in that house. Trust me, it's not for sale."

"With all due respect, Dr. Walker, everything has its price," Bradshaw says.

"I'm sure it does," Leah says. "But not 466 East Lake Drive. I want it removed not just from our files, but from MLS."

"I'm not sure you have the authority to tell me that," Bradshaw says.

Claire makes an exaggerated, shocked face, and taps Rachel's shoulder.

"Let me make something clear to you, Mr. Bradshaw," Leah says, "as my father's executor, I control his seat on the board. Now, I do have to share some decision-making with my sister, but something tells me she'd be more likely to agree with me than you. Since Dad retained a controlling interest in the company, that means I most certainly do have the authority, and believe me when I say, you do not want to test the limits of it. Have we reached an understanding?"

"We most certainly have," Bradshaw says. The sound of computer keys comes through the phone. "The listing has been removed — from our database, at least. Anything else?"

Rachel nods and silently claps. Claire buries her face in her hands and leans forward, laughing. Steven gives a thumbs-up.

"That's it for now," Leah says. "Have a wonderful day." She concludes the call without waiting for a response.

Claire springs out of her seat, waving a fist. "That was badass!"

"Steven, please let me know if you get any further inquiries from Walker," Leah says. "Though I doubt you will. I can't guarantee other companies will leave you alone."

If Never We Meet Again

Early Thursday, Leah drives to the Caine residence to pick up Alyssa. Tim lets her in and gets her a cup of black coffee. She surveys the living room, which is still in much the same state it was a few days before, when she and Alyssa were looking through photos, then walks over to the coffee table, sets her cup on it and starts thumbing through an album. "The chronicles of the Princess and the King."

Tim joins her. "Where are you in all these?"

Leah looks up at him. "I'm not in any of these." She flips to the back of the album where there are black and white and color photos of Leah, as a toddler, with very short hair, in photos with various combinations of her mother, her aunt Margaret, or Paxton. In those with her mother or Margaret, Leah's smiling, or posing, very animated, but in the ones with Paxton, she and her father look rigid and uncomfortable. In one, he's holding her on his hip, but she looks like she'd rather be put down. "Of course, there are the formal portraits. We took one every year to send out to family and friends, and we were all required to look happy in those. I forget which album those are in."

"Aly always said you never got along with your father, but seeing it," Tim shakes his head.

She holds up her hands, "Enough about that. I've been meaning to ask, what did you have planned for your anniversary?"

Tim chuckles. "I was going to take her to this sushi place on Buford Highway where we went on our first date. Then hit the metroplex on 85 for a double feature of *Eat Pray Love* and *Despicable Me*."

"Rather eclectic selection," Leah says.

Tim shrugs. "Aly's been wanting to see both."

There are footsteps on the stairs. A moment later, Alyssa enters, wearing shorts, sneakers and the Braves jersey.

"Are we ready?" she says.

"I'm waiting on you," Leah says. "How are you feeling, Princess?"

"Will you can it with the Princess crap?" Alyssa says. "She's twenty-nine. She's not a baby."

"Term of endearment," Leah says. She takes out her phone. "First things first." She calls up the photo of Claire. Holding up the photo, she moves toward Alyssa. "Introducing CC Belmonte, a local deejay and sound engineer. You know her as Claire."

At the mention of Claire's name, Alyssa perks up, takes the

phone, and gazes at the photo. "Clarabella." She hands the phone back. "So? What are we waiting for?"

The whole way over all she can talk about is "Clarabella" and her enthusiasm level is that of a small child. As they're navigating the Connector downtown, Alyssa seems to recognize the route, and bugs Leah about when and where to turn and which secondary streets to take. Despite not following Alyssa's instructions, the pair make it to Oakhurst in good time and are soon pulling into the driveway of 466 East Lake Drive. Claire answers when Leah knocks.

Leah enters, saying, "Claire" and Alyssa follows, unable to pull her eyes off Claire. "This is my sometimes sister, Alyssa, currently starring as Rebecca Asher."

Claire shuts the front door and turns to face the two of them. Alyssa says, "Hey, babe" and gives Claire a hug, which Claire receives rigidly. Alyssa straightens and looks at her. "It's weird being able to almost look you in the eye."

"You know, you don't look anything like Becky, right?" Claire says.

"I know," Alyssa says. She considers something. "How about this? Whoever you need me to be, whatever you need me to do, I will gladly oblige for just a moment of your love."

"You really did know her," Claire says, with the glimmer of a smile. She moves away from Alyssa, goes to the couch, and crosses her arms. "It's a lovely sentiment. But it had its limits, didn't it?" She sits.

"I don't understand."

"There seems to be a lot you don't know about our relationship," Claire says. "What's the last thing you remember us doing together?"

"We went to the jam at your friends' house," Alyssa says. "I seem to recall having a good time, though I don't really remember many details, especially after the first half of the night."

"That happened the weekend before Memorial Day," Claire says, shaking her head. "We did a lot of stuff after that. In fact, I believe you apologized to Deanna Savage for your behavior that weekend when you saw her at an open mic event in late-June."

"Deanna Savage?" Alyssa says, glancing first to her left, then at Leah.

"The jam was at her family's house," Claire says. "Becky didn't tell you about the Savages, did she? What about Brian and Charlotte?"

"They're the Savages?" Alyssa says.

"No. Their name is Sanger," Claire says. "They perform as

Echo."

"Echo," Alyssa says, more to herself than to Claire or Leah.

"Heard of them but haven't heard them," Leah says.

"Becky knew them really well," Claire says. "She was a big help in getting them recognized nationally. Charlotte wrote a song after Becky died, called Becky Jean."

Alyssa looks to her left, as though listening to someone. Not quite under her breath and not in Rebecca's voice, she says, "That was about Becky."

"Looks like we've found the limit of her memories," Leah says. "She must have last interacted with Rebecca late-spring or early-summer '05."

Suddenly, Alyssa starts singing, "Becky Jean, your words swirl round my head; your face is in my memory. I feel your presence in my stead."

Claire's eyes widen, then dart toward Leah. "That's Charlotte's song."

"Obviously, Rebecca didn't know it," Leah says.

"Obviously," Claire says. "Alyssa's heard Echo."

Alyssa suddenly stops and acts like she's received a jolt, as though waking up from a bad dream, and says, again as Rebecca, "What just happened?"

"You don't know?" Leah asks. "You started singing."

"Did I? I sort of blanked out for a second," Alyssa says. "Aly started singing then I don't remember anything."

"Aly?" Claire says.

"Mini-Mc," Alyssa says. She points to her left. "Over there."

"One of her invisible friends," Leah says.

Claire considers this and shrugs. "Sure, why not?"

"A counselor is supposed to be joining us but she's running late," Leah says. "Given this latest development, I say we should wait for her."

"Forget that," Alyssa says. Indicating Claire, "I've waited five years to talk to Clarabella. I don't need some counselor to tell me what I want to say."

Leah looks at Claire, who replies, "Fine with me." Alyssa gives Claire a long, curious look then joins her on the couch.

"You say things were different after the summer," Alyssa says. "What changed, Babe?"

"We were still friends that summer," Claire says, "and I thought you were past believing there could be more."

"What happened? Why wouldn't we be friends?" Alyssa says.

Claire puts her hand over her face. "Do I really have to dredge all this up again," she says to Leah. She removes her hand and looks between the two. "I never really had much chance to get over it, since Becky died less than a month later. It seemed harsh staying mad at her under those circumstances."

Alyssa looks at Leah. "I've got to know."

"I hate to put you through this, Claire," Leah says, "but if you could tell us what happened, it would be a big help."

Claire takes in a deep breath and lets it out slowly. "Okay. It was early November of '05."

Rebecca tosses her bag into the back seat of her copper-colored Mini Cooper and sets her computer on the seat beside it. She climbs into the driver's seat and puts on the seatbelt, then starts the car. Earlier, she put the finishing touches on a harsh review of the film festival she had attended and posted it to her blog just before checking out, and she wants to be well away from town before the first officials see it. She doesn't anticipate being invited back the following year. *If there is one.* As she heads for Interstate 85 South, her mind is once again consumed by the situation with Claire, which she left behind. The two have not spoken since, and Rebecca knows she has seriously compromised their friendship.

Their last evening together, Rebecca had straightened up the living room, with much hope for how the evening would play out. She and Claire had been growing closer, and Claire was opening up to Rebecca about aspects of her life before coming to Atlanta. While there was still a lot Rebecca didn't know about her friend, she knew Claire had a very problematic life in Middle Georgia as a young girl and teenager, which prompted her to leave home. Rebecca had a copy of a flyer Claire showed her when they were watching movies at Claire's one night which depicted Claire around age thirteen, looking almost nothing like the woman Rebecca knew, with a header that read, "Missing" and a number in Perry to call if people had seen her. Most recently, Claire talked about Selma, her mother, and how the two hadn't spoken since Selma came to Atlanta to let Claire know Selma's husband had died. It was the same night Rebecca re-introduced herself to Claire; she'd also met Selma then and spent several minutes talking to her at a club where Claire was working the sound board.

Claire opening up to Rebecca was a very promising development as it signaled to Rebecca that she and Claire were establishing a more intimate bond. Tonight, Rebecca was intent on testing the boundaries, and she was certain Claire was ready to take the next step, something she'd always avoided in the relationship.

Rebecca also wanted to capture the evening for posterity and set her laptop onto a table across from the couch, angled just enough to look as though it wasn't pointing right at them, but still able to capture all the action. Rebecca expected there to be a lot of action. She planned to do as she often did when she recorded herself with someone else, which is to have the video recording from the start, but alert Claire before things go too far, letting her make the call if she wanted their encounter on video. Many of her friends did, but enough were creeped out by the idea that she'd made it a policy to ask first. She stepped into the kitchen and brought out the wine she bought for the occasion. Claire wasn't much of a drinker but did enjoy a glass or two of wine or beer once in a while when she wasn't working.

Since becoming guardian of her brother earlier in the year, Rebecca felt her confidence returning. She had recently requested her transcripts from Columbia University be sent to Georgia State, where she had applied for matriculation in the summer or fall. Further, Rebecca and her blog had been attracting the frequent mention of other feminist resources online, and, in October, the blog had exceeded the twenty-thousand follower mark, prompting an editor friend to suggest that Rebecca publish it. Comparing where she found herself to how she'd been when she hobbled back to Atlanta after failing her last semester at Columbia a little more than two years ago, she couldn't believe the difference. There was just one item on her list that wasn't perfect, her relationship with her aunt.

Rebecca had always regarded Rachel as a micro-manager who interfered in everything Rebecca wanted to do. Their most contentious period followed Rebecca's return from school. Rebecca would stay out late, drinking and smoking pot excessively, and wander home loud and belligerent. Her behavior became so erratic that Rachel ended up changing the locks on all the doors and denying Rebecca access to Steven, forcing Rebecca to seek assistance and an occasional couch to sleep on from her friends. One evening, while at a party, Rebecca, heavily intoxicated, found herself engrossed in watching a porno film from the early 80s when something about one of the performers caught her attention. She grabbed the VCR remote and rewound the tape several times before the answer appeared to her. A young actress, billed as Carmen Delectable, had a rather ornate tattoo on her left shoulder depicting the left side of an elaborate heart. Rebecca was very familiar with that tattoo.

Rachel's life in Los Angeles, particularly the late-70s and early-80s had always been a mystery to Rebecca and now she knew why. She took the tape to a friend and paid him to investigate the actress and find more of her work, and he brought her about twenty titles produced over four or five years featuring her. Rebecca amassed as much as she could and showed up at the first court ordered mediation session about Steven with a thick file. Rachel's reaction was not what Rebecca expected.

"I could have saved you the time and expense, Becky," Rachel said. "I'm not ashamed of what's in that file. I was young and made a lot of mistakes which I've paid for dearly, but I don't hide from my past. I speak about it rather frequently, in fact."

Rebecca's friend had mentioned this fact, but Rebecca had been so determined to gather dirt she could use against Rachel, she hadn't listened.

"How do you think Steven will react to your trashing my reputation in open court?" Rachel went on. "He'll be there, you know, since it's his future we'll be discussing."

This was another factor Rebecca had not considered, and most of her resolve began to wane. At last, Rachel made a proposal; she'd step aside as Steven's guardian and not oppose Rebecca taking over, so long as Rebecca did not interfere with Rachel's relationship with Steven. Rebecca pretended to consider this for several minutes, though she knew the moment Rachel said it that she'd agree to the terms. Finally, Rebecca said, "That's acceptable to me".

In the Spring, Creative Loafing did a feature on an organization called Journey From Night, which helps women and teens escape from the sex industry and one of the prominent volunteers interviewed was Rachel, who didn't simply donate her time answering phones or making coffee, but actually did field work, confronting pimps and johns on the street in an effort to rescue exploited women. In her time with the organization, Rachel had been beaten up, choked, stabbed, threatened with guns, and placed on a hit list compiled by sex traffickers. In her interview, she talked about the self-defense technique she uses and teaches other volunteers to defend themselves without harming the other person, and the discipline required to ward off attacks without attacking back.

Reading the article and talking to the reporter, Rebecca realized she totally misjudged her aunt. She'd always considered herself a committed feminist, campaigning for liberal candidates, agitating for a woman's right to choose, calling for tougher laws protecting against domestic violence, advocating against misogyny in the media, but she'd always done so from the safety of her computer console. Rachel's feminism was out-front and hands-on. She didn't just advocate for victims of sexual abuse, she put herself in danger rescuing them. Rebecca made calls and wrote letters to her representatives in Congress; Rachel testified before Congress, and she had also stalked the hallways, confronting Senators and Representatives directly to demand change, parking herself outside their offices so they couldn't avoid her. So far, Rebecca's ego had kept her from fully making amends with Rachel, but recently, she'd started making overtures, such as leaving a voice message inviting Rachel to a family function. Rachel hadn't replied, but Rebecca hoped the proper message had been sent.

Around 6:59, Claire arrived and was admitted by Rebecca who ushered Claire to the couch. Just prior to opening the door, Rebecca started recording.

"Are we staying in?" Claire said, seeing the wine and two glasses on the table.

"For now," Rebecca said. "I thought we'd unwind a bit before figuring out what we want to do tonight."

"Fine by me," Claire said, taking a seat. "Is Steven here?"

Rebecca sat next to her and poured them each a glass of wine. "No, he goes on break the week of Thanksgiving."

"So, we have the place to ourselves," Claire said. "What mischief can we get into, I wonder?"

"We shall see," Rebecca said, raising her glass. "To the night."

Claire picked up her glass, clinked Rebecca's, and repeated, "The night".

After about twenty-five minutes and a few drinks, both were very relaxed and having an animated conversation, with Claire relating several stories about musicians she'd worked with lately, a few Rebecca also knew. They were laughing and sitting close to one another. Claire glanced up at the clock. "If we're planning to go out, we should probably put away the wine, unless you know someplace nearby."

Rebecca moved so she was facing Claire and propped her arm on the back of the couch. "I thought we could just hang out here tonight."

"Are we going to watch some movies?" Claire said.

"That's not what I had in mind," Rebecca said. She leaned toward Claire and tried to kiss her.

Claire slid away from her. "What are you doing?"

"What do you think?" Rebecca said.

Claire looked at the glasses and bottle on the table. "Oh, god, not this again."

"What?" Rebecca said.

"You're trying to seduce me again, aren't you?" Claire said, rising and walking away from Rebecca.

"Of course," Rebecca said, sliding to the edge of the couch. "Why wouldn't I?"

"Remember what I said before?" Claire said. "I've had enough of you trying to get me between the sheets. I told you what would happen if you didn't stop it."

"I thought you just meant I was being too aggressive," Rebecca said. "We've been getting along so well since then. You've been opening up to me. I thought we were getting closer."

"I thought so, as well," Claire said. "Opening up to one another is what friends do. Just because I trust you with certain information about my past doesn't mean I want to hop into bed with you."

"I'm sorry if I've misread your signals," Rebecca said.

"I'm not sending you signals," Claire said. "I'm not interested in you like that, and I know I've made that clear. Dammit, Becky. You treat sex so flippantly. Like it's all just fun and games. Well, I've been raped and there's nothing fun about that. He claimed I was sending signals, too." She stopped and looked away from Rebecca.

Rebecca stared at Claire. "Oh. God. Claire. I had no idea. That makes all kinds of sense now."

Claire noticed a light blinking on Rebecca's laptop, and moved angrily toward it. "Are you recording this?"

Rebecca followed her. "It was supposed to be a surprise. Documenting your first time."

Claire stormed over and slammed the computer shut.

"What exactly are you planning to do with that, Becky?" Claire said. "Show it to your friends? Have a good laugh at my expense?"

"I was going to say something before things went too far," Rebecca said. "I wouldn't record that without your permission."

"But I only have your word on that, don't I?"

"Is that not good enough for you?"

"Okay, then. Erase it," Claire said, pointing at the computer. "Now."

"I will. I swear," Rebecca said.

"Just not right now," Claire said.

"No. I mean," Rebecca said. "I'm sorry. Just talk to me."

"No. We're not going to talk," Claire said. "You've betrayed my trust, Becky — and if you know anything at all about me, as you claim, you know that is the one thing I do not forgive."

She started toward the door with Rebecca following. "Wait," Rebecca said. "Clarabella!" Claire stopped but wouldn't face her. "Remember? Whoever you need me to be, whatever you need me to do, I'll gladly oblige for just a moment of your love."

Claire turned toward her. "Erase the video."

Rebecca looked at the computer. "Sure." She pulled a chair over, turned the computer so Claire could see it, and opened it. Claire walked over and watched while Rebecca deleted the video.

"Empty the trash folder also," Claire said. "I don't want you restoring it."

"I wouldn't do that," Rebecca said, then complied. "Fine."

Claire turned away. "Don't call me. Don't email me. Don't try to see me."

"Forever?"

"For now. I'll let you know if I decide I want to talk."

With that, Claire left.

That was several weeks ago, and Claire still isn't speaking to Rebecca. She waited at least a week before breaking her silence and sending Claire an email, which went unanswered, so Rebecca followed this with a phone call, then a video, all ignored. Rebecca's pretty sure Claire's just deleting her messages as they come in. She knows she screwed up and hopes she will soon get a chance to make amends. It's with a troubled mind that she crosses the boarder back into Georgia.

When Claire finishes her story, Rebecca sits, staring at the floor, shaking her head. "I don't know what—" She stops, glances toward Claire, then away again. "I'm kind of glad I don't remember that."

Alyssa skips around the room chanting, "She's not the fair maiden. She's not. She's not."

Rebecca shoots an angry look at Alyssa but suppresses the urge to say anything. Instead, she looks back to Claire. "What do you want me to say at this point?"

"Why do you have to say anything?" Claire says. "You can see why I might not have been inclined to forgive and forget."

"Yeah, it's getting a little clearer," Rebecca says.

"You were a crappy friend, Becky," Claire says. "I had every right to be mad at you. You pursued me, and pursued me, until I told I was cutting you out of my life if you didn't stop. So, you acted like friendship was fine with you, and I really believed you were sincere, but that was all just a trick, too. I don't feel a bit guilty for not wanting to talk to you because there was nothing to talk about. You violated my trust."

Rebecca stares at Claire for several seconds. "Well this isn't how I expected our reunion to go. I had a lot I wanted to say to try to reconcile with you but now it all seems pointless."

Claire takes in a deep breath and lets it out slowly, then says, "There's nothing to reconcile. Our friendship was over, and you knew that. I may have forgiven you eventually, but I wasn't going to forget what you did. We never would have had the same type of relationship afterward. Actions have consequences, Becky. I'm sorry you died — you didn't deserve that — but I won't apologize for being angry at how you treated me."

Just then, Rachel lets herself in. "Sorry I'm late, but my meeting ran longer than expected."

"Actually, your timing is perfect," Leah says. "We're just waiting for the Hindenburg to pick us up from the Titanic and transport us to Mount Vesuvius."

"That good, eh?" Rachel says.

Rebecca focuses on Rachel. "This is the counselor? Why does she have a key?"

Alyssa skips over and around Rachel. "Counselors always hold the key. Who else would have one?"

Rebecca rises. "You're Rachel."

Rachel looks at Rebecca. "You must be Alyssa — or, should I say, Rebecca? Yes. I'm Rachel Lawson. Leah told me about your situation and I asked if I could observe. If that's okay with you."

Without saying another word, Rebecca goes to Rachel and gives her a long hug, which catches her off guard. "I have so much I need to say to you."

"Wait a minute," Leah says. "She's the fair maiden?"

"I'm not so sure about the maiden part," Rachel says with a chuckle. "But I try to keep up my looks."

They move to the couch and sit, with Rebecca at the opposite end from Claire and Rachel between them. Rebecca takes Rachel's hands. "I'm guessing I never got to tell you how sorry I am for all the grief I caused you, particularly after I got back from New York. I hope you can forgive me."

"There's nothing to forgive, Becky," Rachel says. "You were hurting. I understood that. That's what I kept trying to tell you. I figured we'd eventually be able to talk and work things out, and I'm sorry we never got that chance."

"You were always so patient and understanding," Rebecca

says. "I can't thank you enough for being there when Stevie and I needed you. It took me forever to understand the kindness you showed us. You gave up your entire life to take care of us."

"It was my pleasure," Rachel says. "I love you both. I wish I could have done a lot more for you."

"Just know, that at least by that summer, I was starting to come around," Rebecca says. "If I hadn't made any overtures before November, then it's probably one of the regrets I took to my grave."

"Actually, you did," Rachel says. "You invited me for Thanksgiving dinner, but I was out of town on an assignment that week and didn't get your message until I got back. The very next message was from the state patrol about your accident. If anything, I owe you an apology for not checking my messages sooner. Thank you for reaching out."

They hug again. Alyssa skips over to them. "She's not the maiden, but she'll do for now. Let's just skip to the dragon."

The evening after taking Alyssa to meet with Claire and Rachel, Leah is home when the doorbell rings. She checks the monitor by the door and is met by Claire's face, obscured by a pair of aviator sunglasses. She also seems to be wearing makeup.

"The Phoenix has landed," she says.

Leah buzzes her through the security gate, opens the front door, and almost doesn't recognize the woman waiting there, who's wearing cutoff, acid-washed jeans, fishnet stockings, a black, ripped T shirt with a suede bomber jacket over top of it that's dyed purple with padded shoulders and adorned with chains, and thigh-high platform boots that increase her stature to nearly six and a half feet. Her hair is braided and hangs over one shoulder. She's wearing the aviator shades but takes them off after Leah has a moment to take in the sight. She's wearing makeup that emphasizes her eyes and cheekbones and adds fullness to her lips.

"You said you wanted to check me out in full regalia." She moves to the center of the room, then holds out her hands and turns. "Presenting The Phoenix, Ms. CC Belmonte."

"Phoenix, I like it," Leah says.

"Seemed appropriate, all things considered," Claire says.

"I imagine guys have quite an opinion on this look," Leah says. "You probably scare the hell out of them."

"Men and women," Claire says. "Hetero men spread rumors I'm a lesbian and gay men treat me like some sort of bitch goddess; the women tell people I'm a drag queen."

"Really?" Leah says.

"The worst offenders were Becky's friends," Claire says. "I hated every one of them. None of them came to her funeral, by the way."

"Figures," Leah says. "Want something to drink?"

"Water's fine," Claire says. "I like a clear head when I'm in the booth."

Leah gets them set up and they sit on the couch. At the Asher residence, discussion had turned to what happens next and it wasn't long before meeting with Owen was mentioned. Rachel wasn't happy with the notion of involving him in the situation.

"No, no, no, no," Rachel had said. "If you're serious about bringing him in on this, please give me time to schedule a root canal."

"You're a counselor," Leah replied. "Surely you've dealt with difficult clients before."

"There's difficult and then there's impossible," Rachel said. "Owen's impossible. Besides, I could never counsel him even if I had any concern for him, which I don't. We have too much of a history. It'd be unethical."

By the time Leah left, they'd gotten Rachel to agree to entertain the possibility, but her participation was not assured.

"Has Rachel had a chance to consider the meeting with Owen," Leah says.

"She's still not happy with the idea," Claire says. "But I think she understands the need for it. If she can think of a way to not be involved, she'll beg off, I'm sure."

"I just can't figure out why Alyssa would feel a need to straighten out Rebecca's life," Leah says. "It's been five years, for crying out loud. Steven seems pretty well self-sufficient."

"He was kind of like that when Becky was alive, actually," Claire says.

"There also wasn't a pressing need for Rebecca in any form to patch things up with Rachel," Leah says.

"I didn't get to know Rachel until after Becky died," Claire says. "She's helped me work through some problems I've had with trusting people."

"The two of you seem to have developed a nice friendship out of the situation," Leah says.

"There's always that," Claire says, "even if it never goes any further."

"Would you like it to go further?" Leah says.

"I don't know," Claire says. "I've never thought of myself as gay."

"I didn't either until I got involved with another woman in college," Leah says. "Now I keep my options open."

"Options," Claire says. "That's a safe way of putting it."

"Look, it's easy to get bogged down with labels," Leah says. "If you truly care for someone, what difference does it make if it's a he or she?"

"Rachel and I both have baggage," Claire says. "For me, it's a matter of re-evaluation, but Rachel lost her soulmate and can't imagine anyone who could replace her."

"If it's what you both want, you'll figure something out," Leah says.

"Let's hope," Claire says. "Speaking of Owen, the one thing Becky and I had in common was father issues."

"I'm a member of that club myself," Leah says.

"I gathered," Claire says. "You've not been married, right?"

"Never married; no kids — that I can talk about," Leah says.

"I bet there's a story behind that," Claire says.

"A whole play, if anyone ever bothers to write it up — but not a story for tonight," Leah says. "In some ways, Alyssa was lucky. Her father was the doting and over-protective Daddy who was never too busy to spend time with his little Princess. He remembered every birthday, attended every school function, every track meet — walked her down the aisle when she married the love of her life."

"Why do you refer to him as her father?" Claire asks. "He's your father, too."

"Not really," Leah says. "My father was never engaged in my life. He was too busy raising his other child, Walker Dev."

"Rachel would say you're disassociating," Claire says. "At least, that's what she used to tell me when I talked about my past. Besides, there are much worse problems to have than a rich father."

"True," Leah replies. "I know that I was very fortunate, plus, I had a mother and an aunt who loved me and kept me from becoming too much of a rebel."

"My mother has a special place in hell waiting for her," Claire says.

"So, she's still alive," Leah says.

Claire nods. "I sometimes think she's too mean to die."

"My father wanted a son," Leah says. "Instead, he got a variation on his older sister. He never knew how to deal with me, so he threw money at me."

"Like I say, there are worse ways to deal with problems than that," Claire says.

"The final break between us came when I started my business," Leah says. "I went to his sworn enemy, David Cairo, for financing. Dad never forgave me."

"There's another name we have in common," Claire says.

"You know Cairo?" Leah says.

"Yeah but haven't seen much of him since the early aughts," Claire says. "Especially after he ditched the venture capital business and went out on his vision quest or whatever."

"Not many people have seen him since then," Leah says. "Last I heard he was digging wells in Africa. How do you know him?"

"Before anyone cared who he is, I had an apartment above his, in Druid Hills," Claire says.

Leah nods. "Strange how fate brings people together."

"Like Becky and Alyssa," Claire says. "Odd coincidence, them having the same birthday."

"Same birthday, same hospital. Lots of odd coincidences surrounding this situation," Leah says.

"Do you believe in the hand of fate?" Claire says.

"Not as a guiding force," Leah says. "More as obstacles encountered as we're navigating our way through life. It's how we react to them that determines the course of our lives."

"Did you ever make peace with your father after Cairo?"

"Never," Leah says. "Of course, my situation doesn't come close to what it sounds like you went through, and you not only survived, you overcame it and thrived. That says a ton about the type of person you are."

"Thanks," Claire says. "Truth is, Becky only knew half the story. Someday, maybe I'll fill you in."

"You'd trust me that much?" Leah says. "You hardly know me."

"I can't say what it is, but I feel a kinship with you," Claire says. "I feel like I can trust you."

"Thanks for saying that," Leah says. "I know trust doesn't come easy for you. What's your assessment of Alyssa's recreation of Rebecca?"

"She does act like her," Claire says. "But the Becky I knew was a lot more vulgar, she smoked and drank a lot, and was always hitting on me and flirting with other women, even when we were out somewhere."

"You mentioned her friends," Leah says. "What type of friends did she attract?"

"Mostly people she knew in high school," Claire says. "Outcasts like she considered herself to be. I'd refer to them as hangers-on more than friends. If she'd had the chance to follow through on her plans to return to school, I'm convinced she'd have ditched most of them."

"When I asked Alyssa what this was all about, she said connections needed to be made," Leah says.

"What connections?" Claire asks.

"Another cryptic reference," Leah says. "She mentioned something about literature."

"Writing," Claire says. "Another reference to the hand of fate, perhaps."

"Alyssa's never been a hand of fate type person either," Leah says. "Our mother taught us to live in the here and now and not obsess over the past or what might happen."

"Your mother sounds very sensible," Claire says. "By the way, I saw Dan the other night, and asked him about you. He wants you to come to a show sometime."

"Did he say anything about me performing?" Leah asks.

"He said you were better than you thought," she says.

"He always said that," Leah says. "He would never acknowledge that he was the main reason we got invited places. He always said it was the dynamic we generated."

"Comedy's not very welcoming to women," Claire says. "Like just about every other industry, in fact."

"That wasn't my problem. I just couldn't connect with the audience."

"Why was that?" Claire says.

"Have you done Meisner?" Leah asks.

"We've touched on it but haven't delved into it," Claire says.

"The whole idea is to get out of your head and respond to the other actor, and I could never quite get there," Leah says. "Dan would refer to me always being Leah. You could say the whole idea behind our excursion out west after my mother died was one massive Meisner exercise that in my view failed."

"Why do you say that?" Claire says.

"Because, in every situation, I'm always myself," Leah says. "Despite what he said, Dan knew I wasn't any good. Our whole act consisted of him randomly pulling me out of the audience, and me acting clueless. People laughed but the humor came from his attempts to improvise around me."

"I bet that was hilarious," Claire says. "He's great at reacting."

"It was," Leah says. "But when I'd go to the after parties, people were surprised to find I was the same in person as onstage, because I wasn't acting."

"He said you two went out for a while," Claire says.

"He went out with me and Dottie both at different times," Leah says. "Long before he moved in. In fact, he and Dottie went out longer. I wasn't very responsive in that department, either."

Claire looks at the clock. "Looks like I need to hit the road. I go on in an hour." She rises. "Hey, if you want to hear my set, I can get you in the club. VIP lounge, cheap drinks, the works."

"Who else will be there?" Leah says.

"Rappers, singers, music professionals, entertainment crowd," Claire says.

"They have websites, right?" Leah says.

"Most do," Claire says.

"Might be able to drum up some business," Leah says. She indicates her clothes. "Would this look work?"

"Absolutely," Claire says. "The club's come as you are."

"Perfect," Leah says.

They ride to the club in Buckhead in Claire's Jeep, and Leah settles into the VIP lounge. A short while later, the intro to "Mr. Roboto" starts to play, and Claire steps onto a lift that takes her up to the deejay booth, where she's introduced as The Phoenix and starts her set with "Blue Monday" by New Order, then segues into a variety of 80s, 90s, and early millennial house numbers interspersed with jazz and rock tunes, like "Smooth Operator" by Sade and "Even Flow" by Pearl Jam. Leah enjoys the mixes and makes a number of contacts with artists looking to protect their online assets. Afterward, they head over to Claire's house in Ansley Park, where they're greeted at the door by her overly excited Yorkshire terrier, Sebastian. Claire changes clothes and they talk for another hour or so, then she drives Leah back to her townhouse.

For the first time since their situation began, Rebecca finds herself totally alone with Alyssa for an extended period of time. Leah isn't available, and Tim has to work, and they both decide Alyssa, as they call her, can manage on her own a few hours, particularly since she has no means of going anywhere. Rebecca has been sitting at a table, watching as Alyssa assembles a massive jigsaw puzzle, which appears to depict a large family-style portrait with many people of varying ages. Rebecca can identify Alyssa, Tim, Leah, Rachel, Steven, and Claire, but they're not connected as there are still many pieces missing. There also appear to be others Rebecca does not recognize or whose faces haven't yet been filled in, a black woman in a wheelchair, a tall, lanky teen wearing a baseball uniform, two women in their late-teens or early-twenties who look like sisters, with a young girl around five or six. A short while ago, Alyssa became bored with the puzzle, and started playing with some dolls, a man and a woman, both dressed professionally.

"Rosie, I'm not that type of lawyer," Alyssa has the man say in an exaggerated authoritative voice. "I don't handle custody cases."

"Don't worry about it, Marcel," she says, using a comical woman's voice. "Just make it sound legal. It won't have to hold up in court."

Rebecca tunes this out and again contemplates the situation she finds herself in, existing and not existing simultaneously. She's certain she's here; she thinks, reasons, and responds as herself, and yet, all it takes is one look in the mirror to show her she's not who she believes herself to be. If she is really Alyssa, then why does she feel so much like Rebecca? Try as she might, she still can't make sense of it all. At last, she resorts to what has proven to be her least successful tactic, quizzing Alyssa about her memories.

"Tell me about your sister," Rebecca says.

Alyssa sets the dolls on the table. "What do you want to know?"

Against her better judgment, Rebecca says, "Anything you want to tell me, in whatever format you wish to tell it."

Alyssa considers this, wearing a half smile, then rises and goes to the middle of the room, standing with her hands folded in front of her, as though giving a presentation to class. "This is the story of the sorceress who became a goddess, by Alyssa Ruth Walker." She skips over to Rebecca and crouches down, leaning forward and taking on the cadence of a story-teller from a children's show. "Once upon a time, there was a wise king with two daughters, a beautiful princess he cherished and her elder sister he ignored. And when the king lost his queen, he turned against the sister and banished her from his kingdom. She went forth into the world and acquired vast knowledge and became a powerful sorceress. She could pass through locked doors, peer into the lives of anyone, anywhere, and she could command the dead to speak."

"You're the princess," Rebecca says. "We've established that. The king must be your father."

Alyssa giggles. "Le Roi."

Rebecca thinks about it. "So, the sorceress has to be—"

"Yes," Alyssa says, "she has to be."

Leah appears, clad in armor with a long, flowing red cape, and holding a sword. Rebecca says, "How does she go from a sorceress to a goddess?"

"The reverse of how Deborah went from being a goddess to a prophet in Judges," Alyssa says. "Recognition. Acknowledgement. Do you want to hear the story or not?"

Rebecca nods. As Alyssa speaks, the image of Leah takes the role of the goddess dealing with the shadowy figures of the other characters. "The Goddess Ashera appeared before the high priestess disguised as a young maiden seeking knowledge. Over time, the priestess recognized her for the goddess and asked for a miracle; the priestess was barren and desired a child. There was, nearby, a shepherdess tending her flocks. Ashera touched this woman and instantly, she was with child. When her time came, the shepherdess gave birth to the Star Childe and as instructed by the goddess delivered her to the priestess to raise as her own. When the Star Childe was of age and the priestess was near death, the priestess placed a veil on the Star Childe and summoned the novice high priestess, instructing her to never lift the veil. But once the high priestess was gone, the novice removed the veil and saw the Star Childe for who she truly was, so they set out from the west, toward the rising sun, to the temple of the goddess so the Star Childe could reclaim her birthright."

"What does this have to do with your sister?" Rebecca says. "She doesn't have children."

"It's the story of a mother, and another," Alyssa says. "Wrapped up in the tale of a tragic artist." She crawls onto the couch beside Rebecca and whispers in her ear, "23 May 1969: The Star Childe appeared to me in a vision accompanied by two angels. I now know my purpose." She rises and skips to the middle of the room.

"You're seeing things that haven't happened yet, aren't you?" Rebecca says.

"Some have, but they're pieces of the larger puzzle that haven't been revealed yet," Alyssa says.

"What else can you see?" Rebecca asks.

Alyssa looks up and turns with her hands outstretched. "Everything."

"What happens to me when this is over?" Rebecca says. "Do I just blink out into nothingness?"

"Your fate was determined before you were born," Alyssa says. "You've had a few short hops lately. Last time you killed yourself; this go 'round a truck did it for you. But next time." She laughs. "Next time you'll be around for a while."

"What do you see?"

"You'll be known as Leah Rebecca," Alyssa says. "You'll again be a writer, and you'll become a world traveler to satisfy your wandering soul. You'll live a very long life, well into the next century."

"Leah Rebecca?"

Alyssa nods. "You love your brother. That won't end. He'll be a better father to you than Owen ever was."

"Father?" Rebecca says.

"In time," Alyssa says. "When he meets the Star Childe."

"Who is this Star Childe you keep bringing up?" Rebecca says. "What role does she play in all this?"

"None," Alyssa says. "We exist before she enters the story. I can't even see her face, though I know it so well."

"You and those damn riddles," Rebecca says. "Your mother was right. You should speak plainly."

"Aly, you've said enough," the Voice says.

"Oh good, another country heard from," Rebecca says. "You know, you're not much help either."

"You're here to help us," the Voice says, "not the other way around. Aly, what's next?"

Alyssa stands and announces, "The Angel of Mercy has an audience with the Goddess. In five, four, three, two..."

Rachel has invited Leah over to her home in Dunwoody for a visit, and at 6:30, takes a quick look around to be sure everything is in readiness for the informal evening she's planned. She views it as more of an opportunity to get to know Leah, than a further comparing of notes, though topics of mutual interest will most likely arise. They will, undoubtedly, talk about Rebecca, and Rachel wants to give Leah more information on Journey From Night, but there's another person on Rachel's mind to discuss. Rachel has noted Claire's fascination with Leah, and wonders if there's a similar feeling on Leah's part.

Her mind drifts back to Los Angeles, mid-1989. Rachel's partner, Cherise Santiago, was entering the final stages of her prolonged battle with AIDS, experiencing the dementia that would make it impossible for Rachel to care for Cherise on her own, causing her to make arrangements with a local hospice run by volunteers from the Unitarian church. Moved by their kindness and generosity — they were just at capacity, but somehow found a bed for Cherise — Rachel began attending services at their church, and volunteering at the hospice, where she was able to be with Cherise through her last days. Since she and Cherise had been dealing with Cherise's illness largely on their own, Rachel welcomed the care provided at the hospice. Cherise's family had broken off communication with her upon learning of her condition and Rachel had only sporadic contact with most of her family, except her younger sister, Sharon, with whom she regularly talked.

A supervisor noted Rachel's concern for the patients, and compassion for loved ones who visited, and suggested that nursing might be a good profession for her. Cherise died shortly before Owen walked out on Sharon and helping her sister cope with this helped Rachel focus on something besides constantly mourning her loss. Once she had time to collect herself, Rachel enrolled at UCLA, earned her degree in nursing, and took a job with a hospital in Los Angeles. Along the way, she confirmed her passion was for helping people deal with loss, and that became her area of focus. The methods she learned were of major comfort to her niece and nephew when Sharon died.

The same year Rachel made the heartbreaking decision to place Cherise in a hospice, a teenager named Christine Messner fled her home in Perry, Georgia, to take refuge in Atlanta. She'd been physically and emotionally abused most of her life but managed to escape and reconnect with a former teacher of hers, whose family sheltered her and helped her settle the legal issues she left behind. She changed her name, pursued an education, and overcame much of her tortured background, though she continued to carry with her the emotional scars. Rachel recalls the first time she realized who Claire was, in the immediate aftermath of Rebecca's death, when she stopped by to see a friend of Rebecca's, at Steven's request, and was met at the door by a woman whose face she recognized from the church they attended. "Oh. Hello. You're Claire."

"That's right," Claire said. "You're Rachel Lawson. Becky's aunt."

"I am," Rachel said. "May I come in?"

Claire let her in and Rachel told her about Rebecca's accident and consoled her. Claire said that she and Rebecca had a disagreement and weren't speaking to one another, but it was clear that she still felt the loss deeply. She took Rachel up on the offer to talk further and visited her home several times, as well as interacting with Rachel at church, and, over time, they became close friends. While she was able to help Claire come to terms with her grief over Rebecca, Rachel realized there was a much deeper well of pain within Claire and attempted to help her deal with that with far less success.

The enduring disfunction in Claire's life involved her relationship with her mother, Selma, a disagreeable woman with no concern for her daughter. All Rachel knew was that the two had lived apart since Claire went to Atlanta and had almost no contact with one another, other than a few hostile encounters over the years. Rachel attempted to bring them together, but what they learned from Selma about Christine's background only served to further divide Claire and Selma, though it brought Claire and Rachel closer. Now there's Leah, the first person with whom Claire feels totally comfortable besides Rachel and a few other friends she's known for years, and Rachel worries her caution in dealing with Claire's feelings for her may have, at last, driven Claire toward someone else. Rachel is surprised at how much regret she feels at the thought of that. She knows she cares for Claire, but she never realized how much.

Around seven forty, she welcomes Leah. "Any trouble finding me?"

"None at all," Leah says. "I'm reasonably familiar with this area."

Rachel guides Leah into the living room where she has a tray set up with a teapot and some cookies. "I prepared some mint tea for myself. I always find it helps me unwind. I could put on some coffee, too, if that's more to your liking."

"Mint tea sounds lovely," Leah says.

They sit, and Rachel pours Leah a cup then one for herself. "I'm sorry I can't offer you anything stronger, but I don't keep alcohol in the house. I function better without it."

"Not a problem," Leah says. She takes a sip. "Perfect."

"How's Alyssa holding up after our meeting?" Rachel says.

"Digesting quite a bit, I believe," Leah says. "She learned a lot she didn't know about Rebecca. I've concluded the two last interacted early summer of '05, so the situation with Claire wasn't on Alyssa's radar."

"I did have an idea about why Alyssa took on Rebecca's character," Rachel says.

"I'd love to hear it," Leah says.

"It revolves around what Alyssa knows about Becky," Rachel says. "They were born on the same day in the same place. They both lost their mothers in their teens, so there's some identification there," Rachel says. "And Alyssa knows Rebecca died in a car accident."

"I think I see where you're going with this," Leah says.

"We know that the last thing Alyssa did was try to phone Steven, someone Alyssa didn't know at the time. Given her phenomenal memory, she may have retained that throughout the time she was in a coma."

"I can see that," Leah says.

"It's possible she put all those facts together, and given the stress she was already under losing your father—"

"Not to mention the fact that she'd also just found out Rebecca was dead," Leah says.

"Right. All that, combined with the car accident, may have caused her to conclude she's Becky."

"It's a better theory than I've been able to develop," Leah says.

"Still, the fantasy aspect troubles me," Rachel says. "I've dealt with abuse survivors who've built up elaborate alternate realities surrounding the abuse to escape or rationalize it."

Leah shakes her head. "My father was a lot of things, but I'd never describe him as abusive, though he was very overprotective of Alyssa."

"Abuse can come in many forms," Rachel says. "Sometimes it can be very subtle."

"I see your point. Alyssa's a teacher, and also volunteers with organizations that deal with abused children. If something like that was in her past, she's had a lot of triggers. She's never reacted like this before."

"Sometimes it just takes the right stressor. As I say, these are just some theories I've considered having never extensively counseled Alyssa. No one theory matches every case."

"Speaking of questionable parents, Claire wasn't sure if you'd be willing to participate in anything involving Owen."

Rachel shakes her head. "I've never really gotten along with him. Even before he walked out. He was always a little too grabby the one or two times we interacted while he was married to Sharon." She sips her tea. "But, if it will help resolve the situation with Alyssa, I'm willing to tolerate him for an evening."

"I'll welcome your insight," Leah says.

"We can hash all that out later, but for now, I'd like to get better acquainted," Rachel says. She asks about Leah's mother. "From what you've told me, she sounds like a remarkable woman."

Leah nods. "I always feel a little guilty. She gave up her shot at college to raise me."

"I'm sure she never regretted a moment of it," Rachel says.

"She would have been a wonderful teacher; I know, just from all she taught me," she says, "Like I say, Alyssa takes after her. So, you know quite a bit about my relationship with my sister. What about yours?"

"Sharon and I always got along very well," Rachel says. "We

had an older brother, Rob, who died when we were children, so I wanted to be there for her."

"That must have been tough," Leah says.

"Until I lost Cherise and then Sharon, it was the worst thing I had to deal with," Rachel says. "Otherwise, I'd say my childhood and high school years were idyllic. I was the typical overachieving daughter."

"I know a little something about that," Leah says, to which Rachel nods.

"I did it all," she says. "Cheerleader, drama club, yearbook staff."

"Homecoming queen?"

"I was, though I was certain Cherise was going to win. She wanted it more."

"Cherise was your partner?"

"Best friend," Rachel replies. "Love of my life."

"She was with you in L.A. then," Leah says.

"She was."

"So, how does one go from being the homecoming queen to being in porno?"

"It was the seventies, the Sexual Revolution," Rachel says. "Women were empowered to have sex with every guy who wanted to have sex with them, supposedly without shame, but we know how that works in reality."

"Oh yeah. Like guys needed a revolution to want to have sex with anyone."

"Being on the West Coast did encourage Cherise and I to express our love for one another and that was a good thing. We wanted to be stars. Trouble is, we had no idea how the industry works."

"The proverbial casting-couch?"

Rachel shakes her head. "More subtle. We started as waitresses, then learned we could make more in 'adult' clubs. After that, it was easy to convince us to be on stage. We're dancers, right? There were lots of drugs, lots of alcohol. No one ever makes the choice to degrade herself. Sometimes it just happens when you're not looking."

"I get the picture," Leah says.

"AIDS was the wake-up call," Rachel says. "I was told I had it but turns out the clinic gave me Cherise's results by mistake. Imagine learning you don't have AIDS and not feeling relieved."

Leah shakes her head. "It's made you the woman you are today."

"Small comfort," Rachel says. "I'm guessing you took a much

different path."

Leah chuckles. "I was not the homecoming queen. More of a science geek. Not a very sexual person either, though not for want of trying by the guys I knew."

"Of course," Rachel says.

"My wake-up call was Marla Prentice," Leah says. "One of them, at least. She was an instructor who had a reputation for 'initiating' young women away from home for the first time. That's how I met Dottie."

Leah gives her an overview of her relationship with Dottie.

"We all need at least one friend like that, who sees who we are, not who we present to the world," Rachel says.

"Dottie definitely fills that bill," Leah says.

"You have certainly gained a fan with Claire. You're about all she's talked about since you met."

Leah laughs. "She dropped by the other day to show me her deejay regalia and convinced me to go the club with her. She's very good at what she does."

"Yes, she is," Rachel says.

"We stopped by her place afterward and I got to meet her little yap-dog," Leah says.

"Yes. Sebastian," Rachel says. "Are you not a dog person?"

"I'm less of a cat person," Leah says. "But I appreciate most animals from a distance. Alyssa always has cats."

"Well, if you're going to have a relationship with Claire, you'll need to get along with Sebastian," Rachel says.

Leah gives her a curious look. "If, by 'relationship' you mean something romantic, I assure you neither of us has such feelings for one another."

"It's not a problem if you do," Rachel says. "The two of you are close in age. You probably have other aspects in common. I wouldn't want to stand in the way of anything developing."

Leah waves her hand. "There's nothing developing between me and Claire. I do feel some sort of kinship with her, as she put it, but it's not even remotely sexual. I'm not even looking to be in a relationship."

"A kinship," Rachel says. "Yes. I've heard her use that term as well, though she couldn't explain it."

"The one time we hung out she was mixing music in her deejay booth while I handed out cards to recording executives in the lounge," Leah says. "When we went to her house, we talked about you. I am definitely not the one she cares for."

"I'm not so sure I'm what she needs," Rachel says. "We enjoy one another's company, but I'm worried I might become a burden to her at some point."

"A burden?" Leah says. "She thinks you're still mourning for your former lover."

Rachel nods. "She's right about my feelings for Cherise. Not a day goes by that I don't miss her, that I don't wish I could hear her voice, feel her body against mine. But I know she wouldn't want me to spend the rest of my life alone anymore than I'd want her to do so if our test results had come back differently. Just because I haven't found anyone to share my life since Cherise doesn't mean I haven't considered it."

"Then what's the problem?" Leah says.

"It wasn't easy dealing with her illness," Rachel says. "Watching her deteriorate. Knowing I could do nothing to ease her suffering. I wouldn't want to subject anyone to that."

"So, let me see if I understand this," Leah says. "You're not hesitating with Claire because of any residual feelings for Cherise, but because you're afraid of putting Claire through what you experienced."

"More or less," Rachel says. "There's so much difference in our ages."

"I don't think Claire cares about that," Leah says. "Besides, I know women half your age who are nowhere near as active as you are."

"That's very kind of you to say," Rachel says.

"The point is, you knew your relationship with Cherise was going to end," Leah says. "And you had a fairly good idea how long you had. I can only imagine what that must have been like. Do you regret any of the time you spent with her?"

"Never," Rachel says. "I cherished every second we had, even when she couldn't remember my name or mistook me for the nurse."

"Then why should it be different for Claire?" Leah says. "We're not guaranteed tomorrow, let alone ten or twenty years. It's not how long we have. It's how we make the most of that time."

Rachel is looking down, nodding at Leah's words. "Sometimes the counselor needs counseling."

"Sometimes you're just too close," Leah says.

Rachel reaches over and squeezes Leah's hand. "Absolutely. Let me propose something to you. I know you said you're dealing with the loss of your father in your own way."

"That's right."

"Maybe you're a little too close as well," Rachel says. "I propose, when Alyssa's back to being herself, the two of you sit down with me to hash out any issues you might still have. Might help bring you back together."

"I appreciate your offer and will discuss it with Alyssa when she's herself again," Leah says. "But right now, I'm dying to hear more about this organization you work with."

"Journey?" Rachel says, which Leah acknowledges. "I hope you have the rest of the night."

The Dragon

Leah, age sixteen, descends into the basement of her family's home in Buckhead, a box of Lucky Charms in her hand, and sits at the Amiga 1000 she set up. It's Saturday, and Leah is wearing cargo shorts, an oversized rugby shirt with the sleeves pulled up, and white Reeboks. Her hair is below shoulder-length and uncombed. The computers were purchased by her father with the idea they'd be used to connect him to his office or allow him to work from home but, so far, Leah has been the only one to figure out how to use them, so they've become hers to do with as she pleases. Her father still gives her assignments, such as connecting to his office network to post bulletins, or transfer files, but these don't take up a lot of time, so she's free to pursue her own interests, and lately, her interests have included connecting to bulletin boards on the West Coast to learn how to break into computer networks.

She switches on the stereo, and the room is filled with the Thompson Twins, from rotation at WRAS. She sings along with the radio, "Doctor, doctor, can't you see I'm burning, burning."

She opens the cereal and takes out a handful, which she crams into her mouth, then clicks on the modem software and selects a number from the list. The modem makes its wavering and staticky noises as it connects her to a box just outside Los Angeles. She logs in, then begins exploring what's new since her last visit. As she explores the boards, she keeps notes on a yellow pad by the computer. For the past day, there's been a discussion about a "backdoor" someone left on a server in Texas, and Leah's anxious to see if she can get in using it. She disconnects from the computer in California and keys in the number in Texas and waits for it to connect. Once she gets the prompt, she uses the credentials mentioned on the board, and this allows her access.

Four-year-old Alyssa appears at the door, standing on her tiptoes, which she's in the habit of doing when she's not wearing shoes. She has on a long, *My Little Pony* nightgown.

"Leah," she says. "Can I play the bear game?"

"Sure, Princess," Leah says. She pats her left knee. "Want to see what I'm doing?"

Alyssa hurries over and climbs onto Leah's knee. "What?"

Leah leans toward one of Alyssa's ears and says in a low voice, "It's called hacking, so don't tell Mom and Dad."

"Okay," Alyssa says.

Leah holds the cereal box for her, and she takes out a handful, which she eats one piece at a time, while she watches what Leah's doing.

"This is a computer in Texas I'm not supposed to be logging into," Leah says.

"Why are you doing it?" Alyssa asks.

"I think the main reason is because I can," Leah says, "but beyond that I'm not real sure."

"I want to play the bear game," Alyssa says, sliding off Leah's lap.

"All right," Leah says, "it's still there from last time, but use the headphones, okay?"

"I will," Alyssa says. She sits at the Commodore 64 and starts the computer and loads a program with cartoon bears in it, then puts on some headphones. As she plays, she occasionally sings along with the music in the game.

A short while later, Gitanjali Ramachandra or Gita, as she prefers to be known, appears at the door. She's Leah's age, with short, black hair, wearing sandals, cut-off jeans, and a bulky and faded Frankie Say Relax T-shirt. She stops, regards Leah with frustration, and says, "Why are you screwing around on the computer? We're supposed to be going to the park." She glances at Alyssa and says, "Hey, Aly."

"She can't hear you," Leah says without removing her eyes from the screen. "Headphones." Leah looks at the clock. "It's ten forty-two. The park will still be there."

Gita jostles Alyssa's hair, which prompts Alyssa to look up and say, "Gitanjali Ramachandra!" This amuses Gita, who plops down in an overstuffed chair nearby and sighs. "My father's talking about getting an Amiga."

"Is he? My father has no idea how it works," Leah says. "That's where I come in. Have you ever heard of the Arpanet?"

Gita shakes her head. "What is it?"

"Near as I can figure, it's this gigantic network that connects the military with colleges and government agencies," Leah says.

"Why would they need to be connected like that?" Gita says.

"I guess schools that do research need to connect with the places that fund them. I read someplace the Arpanet was built to withstand a nuclear war."

"That's helpful to know," Gita replies with more than a hint of sarcasm.

Twenty minutes later, Gita has shifted in the chair, so her feet, sans footwear, are over the back, and her head is hanging over the seat. "Are you ever going to stop screwing around on the computer?"

"Sorry," Leah says. "Once I get going, it gets addictive." She disconnects from what she's doing and shuts down the Amiga. She rises. "Anyone meeting us at Piedmont Park?"

Gita maneuvers in the chair so her feet are on the floor and puts on her sandals. "I said something about it to Stewart."

"Stewart, the ass wipe who calls you Rama-lama-ding-dong? Honestly, Gita, what do you see in that guy?"

"He's cute," Gita says. "Besides, he said he'd stop calling me that."

"When's he going to start? Monday?" Leah says. Gita rolls her eyes. "Why are you even bothering with Stewart, anyway? Aren't you supposed to be getting married?"

"Not before I'm twenty," Gita says.

"I cannot believe there's a guy in India waiting for you to come over and marry him," Leah says.

"No. Raja's in Canton," Gita says. "His family moved here five years ago."

"Still, what do you know about this guy?" Leah says.

"Our families go way back," she says. "In the town where my parents are from, kids can get matched up as early as six months old if the families are well acquainted. Raja and I were."

"Well, good luck with that," Leah says. "I'm never getting married."

"What about Mitchell?" Gita says. "You've been seeing him for a while."

"He's okay, but creepy," she says. "Always pestering me to come over to his house so he can show me something."

"Like what?" Gita says.

"Oh, take a good guess." Leah takes the cereal and goes over to Alyssa, who's engrossed in her game. She pulls one of the headphones away from Alyssa's ear, and sets the cereal beside the console.

"You're on your own, Princess," Leah says, then bends down and kisses Alyssa on the forehead.

Alyssa laughs. "Okay. Bye, Leah. Bye, Gitanjali Ramachandra."

They go upstairs into the kitchen, where Melinda is sitting at the counter reading the Atlanta Constitution. A Virginia Slims cigarette is burning in a nearby ashtray.

"Is Dad using the Mercedes today?" Leah says. She goes to the counter and takes a draw from the cigarette. Melinda takes it from her, and gives her an aggravated look, then puts it back in the ashtray.

"What's wrong with Margaret's car?" Melinda says.

"The Karmann Ghia doesn't have a phone," Leah says.

"I think he's golfing at noon," Melinda says. "I'm not sure if he's driving or riding."

"Let's just take the convertible," Gita says. "It's such a nice day out."

"Oh, all right," Leah says. "But if we get stuck someplace and can't call for help, don't blame me."

"What's Alyssa doing?" Melinda asks.

"Playing that bear game for the five thousandth time," Leah says.

"I'll check on her in a minute," Melinda says and massages her temple. "What are you girls doing today?"

"Piedmont Park," Leah says. She kisses Melinda on the cheek. "Love you, Mom."

"Have fun," Melinda says.

They take West Paces Ferry across Peachtree, then go South on Piedmont to Monroe. Leah finds a spot along 10th Street and they head into the park with its usual Saturday crowd. As they're passing the gazebo at the lake, a tall man with dark, curly hair, who hasn't shaved for a day or so, and who looks to be in his thirties, approaches them. "How you ladies doing today? I'm Owen." His rural Georgia accent is so thick, Leah could cut it with a knife.

"Owen," Leah says, and gives Gita a look of exaggerated enthusiasm. Something about him seems familiar to her, but she can't place where she might have met him. "We're okay, Owen."

"What's your name, Red?" Owen says.

"Red?" Leah says. She looks at Gita and they laugh. "My name's Joan. This is Bette."

"Nice to meet you, Joan, Bette," he says. "Out for a nice day in the park, are you?"

"Sure are," Leah says. "What brings you out?"

"Oh, you know, just looking to see what kind of trouble I can get into," Owen says. "How about we stir something up?"

Before Leah can respond, from several yards away, a woman with light red hair and wearing dark glasses and a floppy hat calls out, "Owen. There you are." A little, dark-haired girl, about Alyssa's age, runs up to him. "Daddy!"

Leah and Gita laugh again.

"I don't think your family needs any more trouble, Owen," Leah says emphasizing his name. "But thanks anyway."

Owen picks up the little girl. "Hey there, Little Bit."

The woman joins them and says, "Hello. Owen, who are your friends?"

"We're just a couple of girls trying to stay out of trouble," Leah says. "You folks have a nice day."

As they walk away, Leah and Gita burst into laughter. Gita glances over her shoulder. "What a creep."

"Brace yourself," Leah says. "He's probably just the warmup."

Dudley Clyde Asher always had a fascination for flying. While he was still in high school, he started working for a crop-dusting firm near his hometown of Perry, Georgia, flying twin engine prop planes. In the aftermath of Pearl Harbor, Dud didn't wait to be drafted, but marched down to the local recruiter and used his flight experience to sign up for the Army Air Corps, and, in a matter of months, he was in Europe, flying heavy bombers over some of the most hotly contested theaters of the war. Shot down twice, but never captured, he earned the Distinguished Flying Cross, the Air Medal, a Silver Star, and a Purple Heart for wounds sustained evading the enemy while leading his crew to safety after crash landing while participating in the bombing of Dresden.

A few months before enlisting, he married his childhood sweetheart, Patricia Jean Tucker, who learned just after he shipped out that their first child was on the way, which turned out to be a daughter who Patsy named Deanna Clyde. Back in the states after VE Day, Dud put his flight training to good use, opening his own crop dusting business in Cordele. Over the next several years, Dud and Patsy had three more daughters, and Dud taught all of them to fly as soon as they were big enough to reach the controls. His two oldest daughters went to work with the company and stayed after they married and started their families. When Patsy was expecting their fifth in early-1953, she let Dud know this would be their last, and Dud was very relieved when it turned out to be their only son, who they named Owen Monroe after two of his great-grandfathers.

Owen was an exceptionally cute baby with a full head of jet-black, curly hair, and expressive blue eyes, who was spoiled by his mother and older sisters. Just like his sisters, Owen learned to fly at an early age, and by high school, in addition to helping out with the family business, made some cash on the side shuttling people between the various small airstrips throughout rural Georgia. When he graduated, he enlisted in the Air Force, and, like his father, flew missions over Europe, albeit as a cargo pilot. Along the way, he earned his degree in Engineering and, once he left regular service in 1977, he headed to Atlanta to pursue graduate studies. Once there, he joined the Reserves, found work as a pilot for DHL, and, halfway through his first year of classes, met an attractive, ginger-haired undergraduate named Sharon Lawson. They married late in '79.

Dorothy Gage is at her desk in the corporate offices of Delta Airlines in Atlanta. She's been with the company, in various capacities since the late nineties, after working for American Airlines in Boston for several years after she graduated from Wellesley College in 1991.

When she started at Wellesley, Dorothy began a brief but very intense relationship with one of her instructors. It was her first experience with a woman, and she fully committed herself to it, but found the other woman less than enthusiastic at Dorothy's constant attention, breaking off the affair after about a week. Certain that someone had come between them, Dorothy stalked the instructor for several days, until she found her at a coffee house with a scruffy, red-headed girl who looked to be around Dorothy's age. She followed this new woman back to her dormitory, and the following afternoon, after fortifying herself with a bottle or two of wine, set out to show this interloper how she dealt with rivals. The woman, who Dorothy would learn was Leah Walker, met her head on, however, and after a few threats, followed by a good deal of puking, Dorothy settled down and she and Leah compared notes to find they'd both been led on by the instructor.

Dealing with this situation, they became fast friends, and the following summer moved to an apartment off-campus. At times, their relationship would intensify, but, mostly they were just close friends who enjoyed spending time together. Since both were multilingual, they would often converse in different languages, as a novel way to ward off potential male or female suitors when they were out together. Each would choose a language at the start of the evening, and only address the other in that language. In turn, the other would reply with a different language. In the event they encountered someone who could understand them both, they'd invite him or her back to the apartment. Since school, she and Leah have made sure to stay in touch, and usually take a trip together once a year. Since Leah moved back to Atlanta, after MIT, they see one another much more often, though they live a considerable distance from each other.

In her current capacity, she deals with the scheduling program pilots use to book their flights. Each pilot checks the schedule and requests desired flights and times, with the more senior pilots getting priority. Dorothy is able to override the system if conflicts arise, or someone is needed last minute, or if she notes a pilot is exceeding the number of hours he or she is supposed to work.

Her phone rings, and she answers in her practiced corporate monotone. A familiar voice greets her. "Daaah-Teeee!"

"Leeee-Aaaahh," Dorothy says, her voice warming. "You've been a little scarce lately. I was starting to get worried. How are you holding up?"

"Dealing with things as best as I can," Leah says. "On top of everything else, my sister was in a car accident."

"Oh, no," Dorothy says. "She okay?"

"Physically, she's fine," Leah says.

"That's good to hear," Dottie says.

"I'll give you a full accounting once I have a chance to catch my breath," Leah says.

"What's up?" Dottie asks.

"I seem to recall you have something to do with scheduling there, am I right?" Leah says.

"I do," Dorothy says.

"I need one of your pilots for an evening."

"Ooo, can I watch?" Dorothy says. "You know I don't mind sloppy seconds."

"It's not that kind of encounter," Leah says. "I just need him in Atlanta, overnight — within the next week, maybe?"

"That's within the realm of possibility," Dorothy says. "What's my reward?"

"Spa weekend at Chateau Elan?" Leah says.

"It's a start," Dorothy says. "Give me the details and I'll get back to you once I see how many regulations I'll need to break to pull this off."

"Perfect," Leah says. "His name is Owen Asher."

Owen flies into Hartsfield Airport around noon on 20 April 1981, and once he's done with his administrative duties, heads over to Northside Hospital, where early that morning, Sharon gave birth to their first child, a daughter they've mutually decided to name Rebecca Jean, after her two grandmothers. When he arrives, his mother-in-law, who came up from Florida to help out during Sharon's pregnancy, tells him Sharon's sleeping, and directs him to the nursery, where he can see his daughter. There, he notes a man in casual but expensive clothing, with his eyes on one of the cribs. Owen locates the crib labeled "Asher" and smiles at the tiny child in it. "Hello, beautiful. You're just a little bit, aren't you?"

The other man looks in Owen's direction. "Congratulations. Your first?"

Owen nods. "Congratulations to you, too. Is it obvious?" The other man nods. A thought occurs to Owen and he reaches into his jacket pocket and removes a cigar in a wrapper that reads "It's a girl!" which he hands to the other man. The man reciprocates by taking out a similar cigar, which he gives to Owen. He extends his hand. "Paxton Walker."

"Owen Asher," he says as they shake hands. "Weren't you responsible for building the annex at Hartsfield?"

"I had a hand in it," Paxton says. Noting Owen's uniform, he continues, "What do you do for DHL?"

"Pilot," Owen says.

While they're talking, a tall, red-haired woman arrives with a young teen-aged girl who looks like the woman's daughter, with short-cropped auburn hair and wearing a school uniform Owen doesn't recognize. The girl waves at Paxton. "Hey, Dad." They join Paxton and Owen.

Paxton introduces the woman. "This is my sister, Peg." He hesitates when the woman gives him a nasty look. "Sorry. My sister, Margaret, and my daughter, Leah. Owen Asher."

"Great to meet you both," Owen says. Pointing to Leah, he asks, "You excited at having a little sister, Leah?"

"I guess," Leah says. She and Margaret go to the window. "There's Alyssa."

"She's gorgeous," Margaret says.

Leah looks back to Owen. "Which one's yours?" Owen points out Rebecca. "Wow, she's small." She looks at his uniform. "Do you fly planes?"

"I do," Owen says. "Freight mostly, but I'm looking to make the transition to passenger flights."

"That sounds like fun," Leah says.

"The best kind of life," Owen says. "But you're also responsible for the safety of everyone on board."

Margaret puts her hand on Leah's shoulder. "We're going to need to get going. You've got homework young lady."

"We're going to see Mom, right?" Leah says.

"Of course," Margaret says.

They say their goodbyes and head up to the room.

"Quite a young woman you have there," Owen says to Paxton.

"Unfortunately, we've never had much of a relationship," Paxton says. "I've always been too busy." He points to Alyssa's crib. "But things are going to be different with this one. I'm going to make sure she knows how much I care."

"You know, it's never too late," Owen says.

Paxton shakes his head. "Leah's just too independent. She's never needed her father. But Alyssa. I know she's going to be Daddy's little princess."

"I just hope I can always be there for my Little Bit," Owen says. "Give her a Dad she'll be proud of."

Paxton slaps him on the back and says, "I know being a father seems daunting, but trust me, those instincts will kick in and you'll somehow start to figure things out." This eases some of Owen's nervousness. He thanks Paxton, then heads off to find a phone to tell his family the news.

When Sharon informs her in-laws of Owen's departure, Clydie, his oldest sister hops in a plane and flies to the West Coast to locate and confront her baby brother. Owen's three other sisters immediately head to Atlanta to offer support to Sharon, Rebecca, and Steven. Owen's parents, Dud and Patsy can't make the trip, due to health concerns, but let Sharon and the kids know they are there for them morally and financially, if needed. None of this has an effect on Owen, who fills up his flight schedule to stay busy and avoid his sister. Clydie spends several days chasing him back and forth across the country, before heading home at her husband's insistence. Owen forwards all his calls to a crash pad in Omaha, so he can screen out unwanted entreaties from his folks. His response prompts the family to sever communications with him for nearly a decade.

Sharon's greatest fear is that he'll sell the house since, though they both contribute equally to the mortgage payments, it's solely in his name. She consults an attorney to find out how she can prevent that. It's not until the first meeting with attorneys that Owen reveals that selling the house has not occurred to him, since the children live there, and the value has not increased much since the closing. Wanting to fully sever ties with his life in Atlanta, Owen is fine with Sharon getting the property, and agrees to her offer to waive spousal support in exchange for him paying off the mortgage. In time, as the area gentrifies, Owen comes to regret losing the property, but realizes he would not have benefited anyway, since he didn't want to hang on to the place with Sharon and the kids still there.

The person hardest hit is Rebecca, who has always maintained a close relationship with her father, or so she thought. Owen had kindled her love of baseball by taking her to Braves games since she was old enough to enjoy them, and when they couldn't attend, they'd watch them together when he was at home. Owen was also in the habit of spontaneously taking Rebecca, Sharon, and Steven, out for ice cream when he returned from a flight or bringing home treats from his visits to some distant town. After he's gone, Rebecca asks Sharon lots of questions about why, and what happens next.

As upset as she is over the situation, Sharon strives to remain cool when talking to Rebecca or Steven, though she has no good explanation for Owen's actions. Owen was always very popular, especially among women, and on several occasions, Sharon answered the phone to be greeted by a woman's voice asking for him. Owen would take the call, explaining, "It's work." Beyond this, Sharon never noted any of the telltale signs of infidelity. When he wasn't flying, Owen was always at home and by all objective measures played the part of devoted husband and father very well. He always took an interest in Rebecca and helped out with Steven when Sharon needed a break. As far as she could tell, no aspect of their marriage had been lacking. Much later, she finds out about the extra time Owen added to his trips to insure an evening away, or his opting for flights that required a layover in places like Los Angeles or Portland, where he never lacked for companionship.

The following year, Rebecca turns ten and the Braves have their "worst to first" season, heading to the World Series for the first time since moving to Atlanta, and Rebecca gets caught up in every minute of it, taking Owen's place in indoctrinating Steven in a love for the game. Her favorite player is Chipper Jones, and she has Sharon buy her a jersey with his number. It quickly becomes her favorite attire, so much so that she replaces each one as she outgrows it. Over time, she stops hoping Owen will return to help her enjoy the season.

One evening, Sharon takes the kids to Coach and Six just north of Midtown, to get their minds off Owen. Rebecca has on her jersey and the concierge indicates it, saying, "You like Chipper. Think they're going all the way this year?"

"I hope so," Rebecca says.

He looks at Sharon. "Table for four?"

"Three," she replies.

He gives Sharon a sympathetic smile with a nod. "Of course. Right this way."

That evening, and all subsequent evenings, Sharon does all

she can to be a source of comfort and stability for her children. With limited assistance from her family and in-laws, and frequent calls to Rachel for moral support, Sharon resolves to make life as stress-free as possible for Rebecca and Steven, with no way of knowing how little time she has left with them.

Dorothy is at her desk mid-afternoon 31 August, when the phone rings. "Ms. Gage, this is Peterson in Ops. We've got a senior pilot deadheading into ATL from LAX and no one seems to know why. Name's Asher."

Dottie runs her finger along her keyboard to make it sound like she's typing. "Oh, yeah. We needed someone, and I mixed him up with another legacy Northwest pilot. He was airborne before I caught the error. I'm setting him up with a flight back to his base in SEA for the following afternoon. I was hoping no one would notice."

"Hmm," Peterson says. "Know what? If he doesn't make a stink about it, I won't either."

"Hey, free night in Atlanta," Dottie says. Once she disconnects, she dials Leah. "Our boy should be on the ground by 6:30 and find out he's not needed until tomorrow afternoon about twenty minutes later. Then he should be on his way."

"Perfect," Leah says. "We'll be waiting."

"Oh, that weekend at Chateau Elan?" Dottie says. "Make it a week, intensive spa time, and throw in a case of their best Merlot."

"You got it," Leah says. "Thanks DT."

Prior to graduating from Decatur High School, Rebecca was accepted into Columbia University, where she planned to major in Journalism, and finance with a combination of limited scholarships and student loans. Once there, she started writing, for school publications, literary journals, extra-curricular student rags, and also took the opportunity to fully explore her attraction for other women. Late in her freshman year, she became part of a clique of highly progressive lesbians. The women staged shows, sponsored talks, and otherwise agitated for change, both on campus and around town. Rebecca's writing skills served her well within the group, making her an important voice in the movement. Through a friend, she got an occasional column in the Village Voice which she called "The Frantic Feminist". For the first time in her life, she felt free, and unencumbered by the expectations of her friends and family back home and came to believe she could truly make a difference.

One evening, halfway through her junior year, as she returned to her dorm, she was startled by a familiar voice calling her name as she moved through the lobby. She turned to see a tall, middle-aged, well-tanned man with dark, curly hair approaching her. Though it had been years, she recognized him immediately.

"Owen the pilot," she said to him, using her mother's derogatory term for him. "What the hell are you doing here?"

"Hello, Little Bit," he said.

Rebecca shook her head furiously. "No. Don't you call me that. Don't you ever call me that again. You gave up your right to call me that."

"Becky, I'm sorry," he said.

"Sorry?" she said. "You ran out on us, left us to fend for ourselves while you're off being a swinging single in Tacoma, and all you can manage is sorry? Oh, by the way, Mom's dead. Don't know if you'd heard."

"I guess I deserve that," Owen said.

"You guess?" Rebecca said.

"Becky, please, I just want to talk," he said, "to try to make amends."

"No. No. Unacceptable," she said. "You think you can ditch out on your responsibilities then just waltz back in and resume playing Daddy?" She stormed away from him, then swung back around and screamed, "To hell with you, Owen. Just hop back in your damn plane and fly the hell out of here."

The confrontation had drawn a small crowd. The dorm manager appeared and said, "Is everything okay?"

Rebecca hurried to him and said, "No." She pointed to Owen. "This man's stalking me. Call the cops."

"Becky, you don't have to do this," Owen said. To the dorm manager, he said, "I'm her father."

"Non-custodial," Rebecca emphasized. "You can verify with the district attorney in DeKalb County, Georgia. There's a restraining order against him there, sworn out by Rachel Lawson, my aunt. She's been my legal guardian."

"Sir, you're going to need to leave," the dorm manager said, assuming a protective posture between Rebecca and Owen. Over his shoulder he said to the desk attendant, "Call NYPD."

Owen threw up his hands. "That won't be necessary. I'm sorry I bothered you, Rebecca. I hope we can talk some other time."

With that, he left. After assuring the dorm manager she was okay, and refusing the offer to speak with police, she headed up to her room, still shaking, where she polished off a bottle of wine she and her roommate stashed there. The following month and a half was a blur for her, as she sank into a deep depression, constantly worried Owen would return, and dealt with it using alcohol and marijuana. When she finally sobered up, she learned she had missed her finals and was on academic probation after failing all her classes. Feeling control of her life spiraling away from her, she packed her car, and headed for home.

Every time Alyssa raises her head, the room starts spinning and she feels nauseous. So, she just won't raise her head. Simple solution. It's not easy, though, because Rebecca is sitting nearby, saying something into her computer, her back to the couch where Alyssa is lying. She hears Rebecca say, "I'm probably feeling better than she is." She hears the chair where Rebecca is sitting scrape the floor, and Rebecca walks over and pokes Alyssa. "Rise and shine, Sleeping Beauty." Alyssa remains immobile, trying to ignore her, so Rebecca pokes her again then shakes her. "Oh, Christ. You're not dead, are you?"

Alyssa groans then lifts her head. She looks around and drops her head back onto the couch. Rebecca picks up an empty wine bottle near the couch and takes it into the kitchen. Summoning all her energy, Alyssa rolls over and sits up, and immediately clutches her stomach. She leans her head back against the couch until the spinning stops. Rebecca re-enters and sits beside Alyssa then leans forward with her head in her hands.

"How are you feeling?" Alyssa says.

"Like JFK in the Zapruder reel," Rebecca says.

"How much did we drink?" Alyssa asks.

"There are four empty bottles on the counter, but I think a couple were only partially full when we started the evening, so maybe three, three and a half."

"Do you remember calling someone last night?" Alyssa says.

"I think we called your sister," Rebecca says.

Alyssa covers her face and leans forward. "Wonderful."

"What's up with the two of you anyway?" Rebecca says.

Alyssa shakes her head. "She's a bit older than I am, and she and Daddy don't get along, so about the only time I see her is when something bad has happened."

"I have relatives like that," Rebecca says.

"When I was a little girl, Leah would look after me when Daddy and Mama went out," Alyssa continues. "We'd always have so much fun. She'd tell me stories and we'd play games." Alyssa leans on her elbows and says, "When she'd put me to bed, she'd always give me a kiss. Right here." She points to the middle of her forehead. "Then she'd tell me to lie down and she'd make up a story. Usually it was about a princess."

"That's what she called you on the phone," Rebecca says. "Princess."

Alyssa laughs. "Daddy called me that when I was a child, but Leah's the only one who still does. Sometimes it really makes me mad."

"Why don't you tell her to stop?" Rebecca says.

"I have but no one makes Leah do anything she doesn't want to do," Alyssa says. "That's what I admire about her. She's her own woman. When she wants something, she goes out and gets it. It's probably why she and Daddy don't get along. They're too much alike." Alyssa smiles warmly. "Besides, I sometimes like it when she calls me Princess. It reminds me of how things were before she went away to school. You and Steven sound like you have a great relationship."

Rebecca waves her hands, dismissively. "Please. I could write a book about my family's disfunction. Starting with Owen the pilot."

"It's just unbelievable that he'd leave like that," Alyssa says. "Daddy's always supported me. Sometimes too much."

"What do you mean?" Rebecca says.

"Don't get me wrong," Alyssa says. "I love Daddy, and we've always had a great relationship, but sometimes, he can be a little too overprotective. Like when Mama died. He wouldn't let me go to her funeral."

"Are you serious?" Rebecca says. "Weren't you, like, ten or something?"

"I was," Alyssa says. "My sister and my aunt told him I needed to be there, but he wouldn't listen."

"Stevie was ten when our Mom died," Rebecca says. "I couldn't imagine him not being there."

"My aunt was great about it," Alyssa says. "She told me stories about Mama in college, and we put together this giant jigsaw puzzle — my aunt, Peg, loved jigsaw puzzles — but I wish I could have said goodbye."

"My aunt was good enough to come here and watch over Stevie and me when my mother died and all I've done is bring her grief."

"You going to talk to her about it?" Alyssa says.

"I should, but I'm kind of embarrassed about it," Rebecca says. "I mean, I know she'd probably understand, but it doesn't make it any easier."

"You've got to start somewhere," Alyssa says.

"It's good talking to you again," Rebecca says. "Maybe we should do this more often than every five years."

"That would be awesome," Alyssa says. "But you know how it will be. I'm about to head off to grad school and you've got your life. We'll promise to stay in touch like before, but something will happen and before we know it, we'll wonder where the time went."

"Still, let's agree to remember each other in five years," Rebecca says. "If one of us does, whoever remembers will look up the other. Deal?" Rebecca extends her hand.

"Deal," Alyssa says, shaking Rebecca's hand.

Steven and Leah are conferring in the living room of the Asher residence, early evening of August 31st. Rachel and Claire are seated on the couch. The phone rings and Steven answers. "Yeah, Dad. Okay, great. See you then." He puts down the phone and tells Leah, "Your friend was dead on. Dad says he's getting on MARTA and will phone when he gets to East Lake."

"Perfect," Leah says. "Alyssa and Tim should be here well before that." The doorbell rings. "Or, even sooner."

Steven lets in Tim and Alyssa, who's still wearing the Braves jersey. She looks around. "Take me to the pilot!"

"He's on his way," Steven says. "Becky's room is at the top of the stairs. First door on the right. That's probably the best place to hang out when Dad gets here."

Rachel shakes her head. "I cannot believe I agreed to this. I'm willing to wait upstairs until he leaves also."

"We're going to need you here," Leah says. "In the remote chance that any of this starts to make some kind of psychological sense." She surveys the room, and says to Steven, "Once we get him here, defer all questions to me."

"Not a problem," Steven says.

They chat for nearly an hour, with Alyssa constantly getting up and anxiously moving about, when the phone rings again. Steven takes the call and excuses himself to pick up his father. Once Steven leaves, Leah says to Tim, "Why don't you escort Rebecca up to her room, so she won't interact with our special guest until we clue him in."

Tim nods. "Will do." He goes to Alyssa and guides her to the stairs. They ascend and disappear into one of the rooms. Leah turns to Rachel. "Probably best if you not be visible when he comes in either."

"Right," Rachel says and heads into the kitchen.

To Claire, Leah says, "Think he'll recognize you?"

"He might," Claire says. "I sat next to him at the funeral, but we didn't talk."

After several minutes, there are footsteps on the porch, followed by the sound of a key in the lock. Leah looks at Claire and says, "Showtime."

The front door opens, and Owen enters with his overnight bag over his shoulder, followed by Steven. He's Steven's height, late-50s, with curly salt and pepper hair, and cleanly shaven. He drops the bag by the door, then notes Leah and Claire. "Is this a party?"

"Not exactly," Steven says.

"Hello, ladies," Owen says, approaching the women. "I'm Owen Asher, Steven's father."

"Yeah, we know who you are," Claire says.

Leah holds up her hand to silence Claire, then extends the hand to Owen. "Mr. Asher. I'm Leah Walker. This is Claire Belmonte."

Owen shakes Leah's hand. "Please, call me Owen." To Claire, he says, "I thought I recognized you. I met you at Becky's funeral, didn't I?"

"I'm surprised you remember," Claire says.

"I have this thing for faces," he says. "To what do I owe this pleasure, ladies?"

"We're actually here to talk about your daughter," Leah says.

"Becky?" Owen says, surprised. "What about her?"

Rachel enters. "Hello, Owen."

Owen turns to Steven. "What's going on Steven? Why's your aunt here?" Steven starts to speak, then looks at Leah, who shakes her head. An idea comes to Owen. "I'm starting to think my being here isn't an accident. Maybe the airline needs to look into this scheduling mishap a little closer."

Leah approaches him. "Mr. Asher." She pauses. "Owen. I take full responsibility for all the subterfuge in getting you here."

"Who are you and why's Rachel here?" Owen says. "I feel like I'm being ambushed."

"You are, sort of," Leah says. She gives him a overview of the situation with Alyssa. "We didn't think you'd show up if we asked."

"You're right about that," Owen says. "I'm ready to get out of here and find a hotel room."

Steven steps forward. "Dad, trust me, I know this is weird, but it would mean a lot to me if you'd just hear them out."

Owen considers this and throws up his hands. "Fine. Talk."

Leah and Owen sit on the couch, with Rachel leaning against the arm away from where Owen's sitting. Leah outlines the role they hope Owen will play in helping to resolve the situation.

"That's the most ridiculous thing I've heard in my life," Owen says. "How do you know any of this will do any good?"

"We don't," Rachel says. "It doesn't exactly match any known psychological disorder I've encountered in literature or practice."

"That makes me feel much more confident," Owen says.

"Alyssa has this weird fairy tale playing out in her head," Leah says. "I don't know why, or what it means, but she says she needs to confront a dragon. You're the closest thing we could think of that matches."

"Thanks a lot," Owen says.

"A lot of what Alyssa says may only make sense to you," Leah says, "and it may not make any sense at all, but go with it, okay?"

Owen sighs. "If you think it will help, I'll do my best."

"Perfect," Leah says. She rises and goes to the stairs and calls, "Rebecca. There's someone here who'd like to see you."

Alyssa comes out onto the stairs, followed by Tim. Her eyes are glued on Owen as she descends. When she gets to the bottom, she crosses her arms. "Owen the pilot."

Owen rises. He stares at Alyssa a moment then looks toward Leah. "You know, she doesn't look—"

"Yeah, yeah," Leah says. "Just play along."

"Hello, Little Bit," Owen says.

"Don't call me that," Alyssa says. "You've lost your right to call me that."

"What?" Owen says. "That's what—" He pauses and remembers the encounter. "Becky, I'm sorry."

"Save your sorrow for someone else," Alyssa says, circling.

Owen looks confused. "What?"

"You think you can ditch out on your responsibilities then just waltz back in and resume playing Daddy?" Alyssa says, very agitated. "To hell with you, Owen."

Owen is briefly taken aback. "Becky, I'm only trying to talk to you."

"Why don't you just hop back in your damn plane and fly the hell out of here!" Alyssa screams.

"Oh my god," Owen says. "That's what Becky said. How do you know that?"

Alyssa glares at Owen and seems to be waiting for something to happen. "What happens next? I don't remember any more."

Owen stares at her in confusion, still shaken. He looks at Leah. "What is she—" Leah shrugs.

To Alyssa, he says, "Nothing happened. Some guy told me to leave and I left."

"That can't be," Alyssa says.

Tim goes to her and says to Leah, "What now?" Leah shakes her head.

Alyssa throws up her hands. "It didn't work. I'm still Rebecca."

"I didn't think it would," Leah says. She goes to Rachel and motions to Steven to join them, then says in a low tone, "In all the time you were around Rebecca, did she ever have any problems expressing her feelings toward Owen?"

"Not at all," Steven says. "She was always pretty vocal about how she felt."

Rachel nods. "He's right. It's probably the only relationship she dealt with in close to a healthy manner. She might have felt some guilt when she was a child, but as a young woman, she clearly knew where to assign the blame."

Tim comes over. "I think this has gone far enough."

"Not just yet," Leah says. She motions for Owen to join them and leans toward him. "What she said, Owen, what did it mean to you?"

"Those are the last words Becky ever spoke to me," Owen says. "How does she know that?"

"Obviously, Becky must have told her," Rachel says. She leans toward Leah. "That's it, then. She's played out the confrontation with her father."

Leah stares at Alyssa and shakes her head. "No. No, she hasn't."

"You're not suggesting what I think you are," Tim says. Leah puts up her hand, then leans toward Owen. "I need you to listen and listen well. Things are about to get even more weird."

"I find that hard to believe, but what do you need me to do?"

"From what I've heard, there was a time you and Rebecca had a decent relationship." She points to Alyssa. "Right now, she needs you to be the father you once were. Do you understand?" Owen nods. Leah pats his shoulder. "If there's anything you've ever wanted to say to Rebecca, now's probably the time. Trust me, even though she doesn't look it, that woman over there is the closest you're ever going to get to talking to your daughter again." She goes to Alyssa. "I'm sorry, Princess. I was wrong. The dragon isn't Owen. It's Paxton."

"No," Alyssa says.

Leah takes Alyssa's hand. "It's okay, Alyssa. We'll face him together."

Alyssa seems relieved at first, but then her expression hardens, and she pushes Leah away, gently but firmly. "No. She needs to do this herself."

Steven looks toward Rachel and Claire. "That's not Becky."

Alyssa turns to confront Owen. "Daddy, I need you to hear me. You say you listen, but you never really hear me."

"I never meant to hurt you, Little Bit," Owen says. "Truth is, I never really thought about how what I did would affect you."

"When you were gone, I couldn't ask you why," Alyssa says.

"It was never about you, Little Bit," Owen says.

"Why couldn't you see me for who I am and not the little Princess you wanted?" Alyssa says.

"It was always about me," Owen says. "What I wanted. Who I thought I was. I didn't think I could be a father anymore."

"You still treat me like a child," Alyssa says. "I'm a grown woman. I have a life of my own."

"Up until the day I lost you, I thought there would always be time," he says.

"When you were gone, I just kept asking myself if there was something I should have said, something I should have done," Alyssa says.

"Then it was too late," Owen says. "Our time ran out. I'm so sorry, Becky."

"You wanted me to be perfect," Alyssa says. "Even though you stopped calling me Princess, you never stopped treating me like that. I didn't want to be your perfect princess. I only wanted to be your daughter."

"I failed you, Little Bit," Owen says. "I'll never be able to forgive myself for that. You needed me, and I ran away. I don't blame you for telling me to go to hell. It's what I deserved."

"I always tried to be what you wanted me to be, even when I knew it wasn't what I wanted," Alyssa says. "Sometimes I felt I could never be good enough. You made me feel that way. Maybe not intentionally, but you did."

She lowers her head and starts to cry. Owen goes to her, with tears in his eyes, and embraces her. "It's okay. You were always good enough. Both of you. We're the ones who needed to be better."

They hug for several minutes. Finally, Alyssa takes Owen's hands. "You should know, Mr. Asher, as angry as she was, Becky never stopped loving you. She kept all your cards and letters."

Steven looks around at those assembled then says to Owen,

"She's right, Dad. I found them in Becky's closet."

"Thank you for telling me that," Owen says, "little as I deserve it."

Leah exchanges glances with Tim, Rachel, and Claire, then says, "Alyssa?"

Alyssa turns toward Leah, and without a word, hurries over and wraps her arms around her sister. They hold one another for a very long time.

"Welcome home, Princess," Leah says then corrects herself, "sorry — Alyssa."

Alyssa shakes her head. "Princess is fine. I know what it means to you now."

Rachel walks over and touches Owen's shoulder. "You did a good thing, Owen. I can't offer you counseling, because of our past, but if you ever want to just sit down and talk, I'll listen."

"Thanks, Rachel," he says.

Steven motions to Claire and the two of them head into the kitchen to get everyone drinks.

Ever After

The night after the encounter at the Asher residence, Claire and Rachel are at Claire's condo having a bite to eat and discussing the events of the past few days. Once they're settled together on the couch, Claire says, "I know I've been reluctant to open up to the idea of a relationship, but recently, someone gave me a different perspective, and I realize there's no one else I'd rather be with than you. The intimacy might be a little challenging at first, but it's not like I'm that experienced to begin with."

"I think I may have spoken to that same someone," Rachel says. "She made me see that nothing's ever easy in a relationship, but we need to be willing to trust the other person."

"Does this mean you've come to terms with your grief over Cherise?" Claire says.

Rachel shakes her head. "I came to terms with my grief a long time ago," Rachel says. "I was always worried about putting you through something similar."

Claire shifts so she's facing Rachel and takes her hands. "Rachel, you have to know, I'd always be there for you, no matter what."

"I know," Rachel says. "I just never wanted to ask that of you."

"Don't you think that should be my choice?" Claire says.

"Yes," Rachel says. "Our mutual friend reminded me that life is short, and we should concentrate on the time we have and not worry what the future might bring. I love you, Claire, and I trust you, and I'm willing to see where that leads us." She leans toward Claire and gives her a long, deep kiss, then says, "Rumpelstiltskin."

"Rumpelstiltskin?" Claire says, with a chuckle. "I never thought kissing me would elicit that response."

Rachel laughs. "That's not why I said it. If at any point, you feel awkward or uncomfortable, or just want to stop, say that, and I'll know you mean it," Rachel says. "Also—"

Claire puts her finger over Rachel's lips. "Rumpelstiltskin." She laughs. "I promise you, that's the last time you're going to hear me say it."

This time, she kisses Rachel, then rises, takes Rachel's hand and pulls her off the couch. They exit into the bedroom. A moment later, the door opens a crack and Claire drops Sebastian outside and closes the door again. He whimpers, then barks, then circles a time or two and lies down just to the side of the door.

The following Friday, Leah joins Rachel and Steven for dinner, then they head over to The Comedy Factory on West Peachtree for Claire's graduation performance. They sit close to the stage, and once, while Claire is onstage with Dan Barton, he notices Leah in the crowd and starts playing to her. The scene they're enacting concerns a bickering married couple, and Claire takes note of Dan's interest in Leah.

"Oh, I get it," she says, waving her hand and moving closer to the edge of the stage. "There's someone else, isn't there."

Dan acts shocked, and puts his finger over his lips, winking at Leah, then focuses on Claire. "I don't know what you're talking about."

"We come all the way up to this cabin in the woods to get away from it all, and you're still chasing other women." Claire throws up her hands, "You know what? I don't have time for this. There's wood that needs to be chopped."

She goes to a different part of the stage and mimics splitting wood. Dan looks after her, then steps off the stage and takes Leah's hand. "It's okay, darling. She's gone now. We're safe." He looks at her then flips his head slightly toward the stage. Leah rises and accompanies him there drawing laughs and applause from the crowd.

"My husband is not going to believe this!" Leah says with giddy enthusiasm drawing laughs from the crowd.

Dan leads her to a square block. "Sit here, darling. I'll get us some wine."

Leah sits while Dan mimics opening a bottle and pouring some wine. Behind them, Claire finishes chopping wood and turns toward them, holding her imaginary axe. She reacts with shock, then walks over, brandishing the axe.

"Looks like I have more chopping to do," she says.

Just then, a young man runs across the stage and makes a sweeping motion with his hand, ending the scene. Offstage, Dan gives Leah a warm hug. She rejoins Rachel and Steven.

Sandy has been calling Tim every few days for updates on Alyssa's condition. Early in September, she's greeted by Alyssa's voice when she calls, and Alyssa invites her for a visit. The following Saturday, Sandy arranges for her parents to watch the kids and drives to John's Creek. Tim greets her at the door and welcomes her into the living room. As she's setting her bag on the table, Alyssa appears at the door to the kitchen. "Tim was that—"

She stops when she sees Sandy, and throws her hands over her mouth, tears coming to her eyes. Sandy's also crying, and they stare at each other a long moment before rushing to one another and falling into a tight embrace. Tim silently excuses himself into the kitchen, and they hold one another, crying, for a long time. They spend the rest of the afternoon catching up on all the time in between and when they part, they agree to spend as much time together as possible going forward.

A few weeks later, they head over to Stone Mountain to run in the woods, like they'd done in high school. As they're making their way along one of the trails around the lake, they encounter a man with long brown hair and a beard with silver slivers, wearing dark cargo shorts, hiking boots, a faded blue hoodie over a red T-shirt, and wire framed glasses, walking toward them. He steps aside to let them pass, and nods to them before continuing along his way. Alyssa looks back at him, then touches Sandy's shoulder. "Hang on just a second."

Sandy jogs in place by the side of the trail as Alyssa runs after the man.

"Excuse me," Alyssa calls out to him. He stops and turns. Alyssa slows to a walk. "Have we met before?"

"I don't think so," he says.

"You seem very familiar to me," she says.

"I'm pretty sure I'd remember meeting you," he says.

A name pops into her head. "Do you go by Benjamin?"

"No. Not at all," he says with a bit of a chuckle.

"Sorry. I mistook you for someone else," Alyssa says.

"Quite all right," he replies.

"Enjoy your walk," she says.

She turns to go. He looks after her a moment. "You have a nice day — Princess." He turns and starts walking again.

Alyssa stops in her tracks and turns to watch him. Sandy jogs over. "Aly, what's up? Who is that guy?"

"Just someone I met once," she gives Sandy a long look, then hugs her tightly.

"What was that for?" Sandy says.

"For being the fairest of the fair," Alyssa says.

"Seriously?" Sandy says.

"For all the times we missed," Alyssa says. Sandy gives her a warm smile and they hug again, then continue their run.

In early-October, Leah makes good on her promise to Dottie for a spa week at Chateau Elan and Claire and Rachel join them.

Tim and Alyssa have to work, and Steven has interviews with law firms, and can only join them over the weekend. Owen's schedule allows him to be in town, so he rides up with Steven and Alyssa invites Sandy to ride up with her and Tim and she brings her kids. Midday on Saturday, they all head into Braselton, where Owen treats everyone to ice cream at Mayfield Dairy. They then head down to the point on Highway 124 where Rebecca's accident occurred armed with a bottle of champagne, flowers, and other remembrances.

While they're waiting for everyone to arrive, Leah says to Steven. "When you have some time next week, I'd like to meet with you regarding management of my father's estate."

"Management?" Steven says. "That's probably beyond my skills at this point."

Leah laughs. "Actually, I'm managing things and need some assistance with some odds and ends that require a legal eye."

"I think one of the established law firms in town would be better equipped to handle something of that scope," he says.

"Oh, I know," Leah says. "These would just be some occasional filings, or research, just to get your feet wet, perhaps."

"I'm happy to help as much as I'm capable," he says.

"Perfect," Leah says. "Let's talk Tuesday."

Once everyone's there, Leah says, "Not quite five years ago, a life ended near here. I'm sorry I never had the opportunity to really know Rebecca."

She opens the bottle and pours some for each person. Even Rachel holds out her glass. Leah says to her, "I thought you didn't drink."

"I'm making an exception," Rachel says.

Once everyone's been served, Leah raises her glass. "To new friends and new adventures."

Alyssa lays her head on Tim's shoulder and puts one arm around Sandy. "To friends we've lost and those we've found."

Tim picks up the thought, "And to families reunited."

"To life, and love," Rachel says, taking Claire's hand.

Claire says, "To new experiences."

Owen toasts second chances. Sandy raises her glass to family and friends and Dottie salutes the odd journey of life.

Finally, Steven raises his glass. "To Rebecca Jean Asher." They all raise their glasses and repeat, "To Rebecca."